# SUMMER OF THE BFFS

# SUMMER OF THE BFFs

*The wacky, wonderful adventures of Kat, Tiff, Amy, and Hanna*

**Arden Baila and Melissa Baila**

iUniverse, Inc.
New York Bloomington Shanghai

# Summer of the BFFs

*The wacky, wonderful adventures of Kat, Tiff, Amy, and Hanna*

Copyright © 2008 by Melissa Baila

iUniverse books may be ordered through booksellers or by contacting:

iUniverse
1663 Liberty Drive
Bloomington, IN 47403
www.iuniverse.com
1-800-Authors (1-800-288-4677)

Because of the dynamic nature of the Internet, any Web addresses or links contained in this book may have changed since publication and may no longer be valid.

This is a work of fiction. All of the characters, names, incidents, organizations, and dialogue in this novel are either the products of the author's imagination or are used fictitiously.

ISBN: 978-0-595-47683-1 (pbk)
ISBN: 978-0-595-91947-5 (ebk)

Printed in the United States of America

To my Mom for turning my story into a book, my Dad for always believing in me, my sister Morgan for always putting up with me, my grandmothers for spoiling me, and my friends and teachers at Sope Creek and Dickerson for all of their support and friendship.

Love, Arden

Special thanks to four of my BFFs who posed for the cover of my book—Caroline, Heajin, Kristen, and Mikayla. *You guys rock!* I would also like to thank my mom's friends, Jessica and Monica, who also helped with the cover of my book.

Love, Arden

# Contents

# THE ARRIVAL

## TIFF

Tiff squinted at the sun's sharp glare as the limousine hugged the curve and climbed further up the steep mountain road toward a gap between the towering pine trees.

"Where are my sunglasses?" she muttered as she dug through her new purse. Tiff had insisted that her mother buy the large Coach purse for her tenth birthday but now she hated the deep pockets that hid her prized possessions, including her Chanel knock-off sunglasses and her samples of lip-gloss.

"Finally," she mumbled and sighed in relief as she slid the large white sunglasses over her nose and tucked her long straight blonde hair behind her ears.

"Are we almost there?" she asked William, her constant companion for the last five years. William was her chauffeur and drove Tiffany everywhere she had to go.

"Yes, Tiffany," William replied patiently, "the entrance to the resort should be at the top of this mountain, just ahead."

The limo continued to climb up the mountain past unmarked dirt roads that forked from the main road like spooky fingers reaching into the woods. Tiff gripped the seat and felt her stomach quiver as the road rose up steeply.

As they approached the top of the mountain, Tiff saw a huge wooden sign with the words *Camp Cherokee* carved in large green letters. The limo turned slowly through a huge wooden gate that was propped wide open. Tiff shuddered and leaned back into the leather car seat. Camp Cherokee was such a stupid name, she said to herself.

"Why do you call it a resort?" she leaned up and asked William. "You know it's just a stupid camp where my parents want to dump me for the summer while they go to Paris."

"Okay fine, it's not really a resort," replied William. "But it has a lake, hiking trails and horses, so you'll have lots of fun."

"It looks creepy," Tiff whined, "and besides, a resort has maids and waiters. My mom said I would have to make my own bed and clear my own dishes. This is *definitely* not a resort." Tiff crossed her arms with a huff and sank back into her seat.

"It won't hurt you to do a little work now and then," William said softly as he turned into the dirt driveway. "Maybe your parents are worried that you're getting a little … spoiled, maybe."

"I am NOT spoiled!" Tiff sat up and yelled over the front seat. "I just have high standards and I like nice things. What is wrong with that?"

William turned his head to respond when Tiff screamed, "Watch out, you stupid-o!"

William slammed on the brakes and caught a glimpse of a blue baseball cap as someone scampered across the road into a large log cabin.

William turned and looked sternly at Tiff with his sharp blue eyes. "I am not a 'stupid-o' young lady."

"I didn't mean *you* were stupid," explained Tiff. "I was talking about that stupid girl who ran out in front of our car."

"What girl?" William asked looking puzzled. "Wasn't that a boy?"

"No, that was definitely a girl," said Tiff. "A weird girl dressed like a boy. I could see her sports bra through her dirty t-shirt. If that was a boy wearing a bra then I am definitely not staying at this camp! I mean, how weird are these people?"

"That's enough, Tiffany," William interrupted. "I am sure you are right and it was a girl. Now let's get you checked in so I can report back to your parents that I delivered you here safe and sound."

"Yeah, delivered is right," mumbled Tiff as she gingerly stepped out of the car and tried to keep her new pink sandals from sinking into the dirt. "I feel like a UPS package being delivered to someone's door. Just dump me on the doorstep and leave."

## KAT

Kat sprinted up the wooden steps of the huge log cabin, which was the camp's main office. She wondered what kind of girl would show up at camp in a limo. Maybe she was someone famous—like Hannah Montana! Whoever it was, she had better hire a new driver. He almost ran her over!

"Hi, Katherine," said Mrs. Donovan from behind the large oak desk. She was an older lady who ran the camp with her husband and she reminded Kat of her grandmother. "What are you doing back up here?" she asked with a smile. "Are you already settled in your cabin?"

"Yeah," replied Kat as she smacked her gum and pushed strands of brown hair into her baseball cap. "My dad is coaching a football game tonight so he and my mom had to leave. I was getting bored and saw a basketball court behind the Dining Hall. Where can I get a basketball?"

"There's a bin full of balls behind this building. Go ahead and take one, but stay out of everyone's way in the front. We have many campers arriving and I saw you dart in front of that big car. You could've been hit!"

"You mean that big white limo? I knew he wouldn't hit me. I run really fast." Kat turned to run out the door and yelled over her shoulder, "Thanks!"

Kat swung the screen door open and smelled the sharp fresh scent of pine needles. She jumped over the last three steps and landed in the dirt parking lot. Out of the corner of her eye, she spied the limo parked in the side lot. A tall man in a white crisp uniform was unloading a large trunk and some pink suitcases while the girl next to him was shaking dirt out of her sandals.

As Kat got closer, she could hear the girl whining, "This place stinks! It's so dirty!"

Kat continued to walk slowly towards the car when the girl looked up and glared at her through oversized sunglasses. Kat started to smile when she heard the girl say to the man, "Here comes that weird girl dressed like a boy. Hurry, unlock the car and let me back in so I don't have to talk to her."

Kat stopped in her tracks. Weird girl dressed like a boy? Was she talking about her? Kat pushed her baseball cap back and looked down at her new blue Nike basketball shoes, her gray basketball shorts, and her favorite orange Clemson University t-shirt. She wasn't dressed like a boy—she was even wearing a bra! But only because her mom made her wear it.

Anyway, who needs to meet a snob? Kat turned and ran in the direction of the basketball court. In a way, she felt sorry for the girl. Kat had been to several camps before and most of the girls wore just shorts and t-shirts, not a dress with pink and green flowers all over it. Where did that prissy girl think she was … a resort?

## AMY

Amy balanced the small cage in her lap and held it tightly as her mom steered the red pickup truck around the sharp curve.

"Don't drive so fast," said Amy. "You're scaring Rascal!"

"Amy," her Mom said sternly, "how many times do I have to tell you that you cannot take a gerbil to camp. You will need to leave Rascal with me."

"But he's just a baby! He won't bother anyone," Amy promised.

"Rules are rules," Amy's mom replied as the truck chugged up the steep incline. "Now say good-bye to Rascal. I see the camp sign up on the right. And pull your hair back into a ponytail. Your curls are going crazy today."

Amy sighed and tried to pull her unruly red curls back into a rubber band. Her mom wanted to cut her hair short for the summer but Amy had refused. She got her red hair from her father who died last year and she wanted to keep anything that reminded her of him.

Amy took Rascal out of the cage and stroked his head. Rascal was one of her favorite pets. Amy had an aquarium full of fish, four turtles, two birds and a cat. She wanted a dog but her mom worked long hours as a veterinarian and said that dogs needed too much attention. So, Amy bought a gerbil instead.

When she brought Rascal home three weeks ago, she didn't know she was leaving for camp. Her mom's friend had a daughter enrolled in the camp, but she broke her leg skateboarding and couldn't go. Amy's mother grabbed the opening, thinking it would be a good experience for Amy.

Amy just wanted to stay home, take care of her animals, and write in her journal. She patted her backpack and felt her journal tucked safely inside. Her journal would be safe there. Amy smiled as a plan developed in her mind. If her journal was safe in her backpack—so would a gerbil!

She stroked Rascal once more and then, as her mom focused on weaving in and out of the many campers who were scurrying around in the parking lot, she quickly tucked Rascal into her backpack. She left the pocket open for air and tucked some carrots into the other pocket. She then turned in her seat and placed the cage on the floorboard behind the front seat.

"Bye, Rascal," she said, trying to sound sad and lonely. She twisted a strand of her red curly hair and looked out the window at the campground that was bustling with campers and their parents.

"Hop out," said her Mom as she put the parking brake on and opened her door, "and don't worry about Rascal, he'll be fine. The line to check into your cabin is getting long so let's hurry."

## HANNA

Hanna closed her laptop and slid the computer into its Hello Kitty laptop case. She grabbed her backpack and tried to cram the laptop inside with her Game Boy, iPod, Nintendo DS and cell phone.

"I can't fit all my stuff into this backpack," muttered Hanna.

Her mom shifted in the front seat and turned to face Hanna in the back seat as she said, "Honey, you are not going to need all those electronics. You will be too busy outside having fun."

"Mom," moaned Hanna, "you know I don't like to be outside. I don't know why you sent me here instead of that computer camp. Or that space camp in Huntsville—that sounded like fun!"

"Hanna," said her Mom slowly, "we have discussed this over and over again. Your father and I have a lot of work to do this summer with the launch of the new software. We won't have time to make sure you are busy outside getting fresh air and exercise so this camp is perfect for you."

"My life is so FUBB!" moaned Hanna.

"Fubb?" her father asked. "What does that mean?"

"It means," Hanna said grimly, "fouled up beyond belief."

"You'll survive," said her Dad as he parked the car. "There will be days when it rains when you'll be able to stay inside. However, I believe those days are craft days when you will make birdhouses or potholders. I don't believe computers are on the agenda here."

Hanna looked horrified, "You're JK, right?"

"No, Hanna, he's not kidding," her Mom said as she grabbed her purse and opened the car door. "And save those silly text codes for when you get back home."

Hanna pushed her headband through her straight, shiny black hair and slid on her backpack as she slowly emerged from the car. She looked around in dismay. It looked like something from a book she read in third grade called *Little House on the Prairie*.

Hanna would have never survived pioneer times like Laura Ingalls. She needed her modern conveniences. Hanna sighed as she looked around and realized that the only thing new at this dismal place was her parent's white BMW!

"Mom," whispered Hanna, "this is so NFM. I really don't want to stay here! Take me home and I promise to swim laps in the pool or jog two hours a day. I even promise to...."

"Sweetie," her mother interrupted as she put her arm around Hanna's shoulder, "just give it a chance, okay?"

"Besides," said her father as he grinned and rumpled her hair, "we need some new potholders."

# The Cabin

**TIFF**

Well, there was no backing out now. William had signed all the paperwork in the main office and he was now huffing and puffing as he hauled Tiff's trunk into the cabin.

Tiff stood at the door of Cabin #3 and peaked inside. It was dark and smelled like one of the tiny pine trees people hang from the rear view mirror in their car. There were two bunk beds on opposite sides of the cabin. One bottom bunk was already made up with a comforter and sheets printed with basketballs.

Tiff had a horrible thought and whispered to William, "Oh, no! That crazy boy-girl person is staying in this cabin. Look at that bed!"

William looked up from the heavy trunk and wiped sweat from his forehead. "I am sure she is nice," he replied. "Pick your bed so I can help you make it."

Tiff stood glued to the doorstep and continued to look around the dim room. To her left and right were the bunk beds. There was a large blue round rug in the middle of the room and a single white sink mounted to the back wall. A simple wooden desk and a chair were next to the sink with a large window above the desk. Tiff could feel a soft breeze stirred by the paddle fan that turned slowly with a soft clicking noise from the center of the ceiling.

As she continued to stare at her new surroundings, a slight movement to the right caught her attention. She turned her head and saw, crawling up the wooden doorframe, the biggest black spider she had ever seen! Tiff screamed and jumped back, lost her balance on the steps and tumbled backwards.

## KAT

Kat was bounding up the steps of her cabin when that movie star wanna-be girl came tumbling backwards right on top of her! They both fell and landed in the dirt at the bottom of the steps.

Kat jumped up and wiped the dirt off the back of her shorts. The tall man who had been driving the limo ran out of the cabin and lifted the prissy girl off the ground. The girl was crying hysterically about some poisonous spider. Kat looked at the doorframe where the girl was pointing and saw the spider.

"Do you mean this little ol' thing?" Kat asked as she reached towards the doorframe. "This is a wood spider. It's not poisonous at all."

Kat gently put the tiny spider into the palm of her hand and held it out to the trembling girl. "Here, you can touch it. It won't hurt you."

The girl shrunk back in horror, ran back into the cabin and flopped down on the other bottom bunk in tears.

Kat breathed a sigh of relief when she saw that she had not picked the bed above hers. She wouldn't want that hysterical princess sharing a bunk with her! Kat flicked the spider off her hand into the bushes and ran back down the steps toward the basketball court. Better come back in a little while when the princess had calmed down.

## AMY

As Amy approached the cabin with her mother, she could hear someone crying. She looked anxiously up at her mother who took her hand and squeezed it gently.

"Someone is probably just homesick already," said her mom softly. "Let's just peek inside and see what is going on."

As they stepped inside, their eyes adjusted to the dim room and they spotted a blonde girl crumpled on a bottom bunk crying. A tall man in a white uniform was leaning over and patting her back.

"Tiffany," he was saying softly, "it was just a spider. I know it scared you but it is gone and you are fine. Sit up and go wash your face."

"I hate this place," the girl wailed and hid her face again in the bed.

The man looked up and smiled at Amy and her mom as they stood in the doorway. "Hello, don't mind us. Tiffany is quite a drama queen, but she'll be fine in a minute."

Amy watched as the tall man with dark hair and friendly smile stood up, straightened his cap, and held out his hand to Amy's mom. "I'm William Orr, Tiffany's chauffeur."

Amy saw her mom raise her eyebrows a bit as she replied, "I'm Vicky Cartwright and this is my daughter, Amy."

Amy smiled shyly at the man and then glanced again around the room. She wanted her mom to stay but she also needed her to leave so she could sneak Rascal out of her backpack. She spotted the bottom bunk bed with the basketball comforter and carefully put her backpack on the top bunk.

Her mom placed her trunk at the end of the bunk bed, took out a set of sheets and started to make up the bed. Amy didn't bring a comforter but she had her soft brown wildlife blanket with deer, wolves and bears.

Amy felt safe wrapped in her blanket. Sometimes she would pretend that wild animals would protect her if she ever got lost in the woods. She knew it was kind of silly but ever since her dad died in a boating accident last year she got scared easily and needed to surround herself with things that made her feel safe, like her blanket, her pets and her journal.

There were many nights when Amy would lay in bed and cry as this other girl was doing. But she would never cry because of a spider, but because she missed her dad. Now she would be missing her mom, too.

Amy saw that her mom was finished making the bed. She gave her a big hug and whispered, "Bye, Mom. I will miss you so much. Promise me you won't work too hard while I am gone!"

Amy's mom hugged her back tightly and then kissed the top of her head. "I'll miss you too, honey. Have fun and try to make some new friends. And stay away from any wild animal you might find in the woods, okay?"

"I promise," she whispered in her Mom's ear as she crossed her fingers behind her back. She knew this was a promise she could not keep. After all, she was more scared of making new friends than any animal in the woods.

## HANNA

Hanna followed her mom and dad to her new home for the next two weeks. She couldn't believe that she was going to stay in an old log cabin with no Internet access or even a television! At least her iPod was loaded with her favorite tunes and her Game Boy with the latest hot games.

Hanna shifted the heavy backpack to a more comfortable position and stepped into the cabin. No comfort here—just a lot of wood. There was wood on the walls, wood on the floor, even wood on the ceiling! There was no wall-to-wall carpet, no lamps, no comfy chairs, and no big screen television. Hanna glanced around the room to locate an electrical outlet.

"Dad," exclaimed Hanna, "I don't see an outlet next to either one of the bunk beds. How do I plug in my laptop? This is totally unacceptable!"

"Hanna," her mom said, "I am sure there is an outlet somewhere in this room. Let's get you settled in first. Look, there is one bunk bed left—the top one over here."

Hanna's mom headed to the empty bed that was above a blonde girl who looked like she had been crying. The girl wiped her eyes and looked curiously at Hanna. Sitting on the other top bunk was another girl with long red curly hair. She twisted a long curl around her finger and barely looked at Hanna.

Great, thought Hanna. I have weird cabin mates.

As if she was reading her mind, the blonde girl said to Hanna, "This place is weird, isn't it? I want to go home but I think we're stuck here for the next two weeks."

Hanna smiled at the girl and, as she placed her backpack on the top bunk, she whispered, "I don't blame you for crying—this place could make anyone cry!"

The blonde girl smiled and said, "My name is Tiffany but everyone calls me Tiff."

"I'm Hanna."

Tiff pointed to Amy and said, "That girl doesn't talk but I think her name is Anna."

"My name is Amy," the girl said softly. "And I do so talk.... when I need to."

"See," said Hanna's mom, "you've made some friends already. Give me and your dad a hug and we will be on our way."

As Hanna hugged her parents, she saw Tiff giving a tall man a hug goodbye. The three girls found themselves alone in awkward silence when the door flung open and in ran another girl.

"Hi," she said breathlessly as she smacked a large wad of gum and shoved her hair back into a baseball cap. "I ran all the way from the lake. This place is amazing! There are canoes, paddleboats, and stables with lots of horses. And, they have a Blob!"

Hanna looked at the newest addition to their cabin who stood at the door with a large grin on her face.

A blob? What in the world could that be? Whatever it was, she would stay far away from it. Hanna sighed and wished that she could crawl into her computer and e-mail herself back home where she belonged.

# THE COUNSELOR

## LILY

Lily walked from the camp office to Cabin #3. She was anxious about meeting her four new campers. This was her first time as a Lead Counselor and she was a little nervous. Lily had been coming to summer camp every year since she was ten years old. Now that she was sixteen, she was old enough to be a Lead Counselor.

She had certainly paid her dues. Two years as an Assistant Counselor, which meant you were a servant for the lead counselors. She had to serve them food, wash their dishes and the most disgusting job of all—clean the outhouses, gross! But, no more, because now she was the head honcho, the leader of the pack—the boss!

Lily was small for her age so she knew that she would have to work extra hard to gain the respect of her campers. Some twelve year olds were taller than she was! However, being small wasn't too bad. In her ballet recitals, Lily was the one who the male dancers picked up over their heads. Lily loved being twirled high across the stage! Lily was missing a lot of ballet practice this summer since she was a counselor so she would do her stretches every day in the Yoga classes offered to the campers.

Lily arrived at the cabin door and took a deep breath. She opened the door and found one camper standing in the middle of the room with the three other campers sitting on their bunks with long faces.

"Hi," she said trying to sound cheerful. "I'm Lily, your Lead Counselor. I'm really happy you are here and I can't wait for us to get to know each other. Have all of you met each other already?"

The girl with blonde hair stood up from her bed and said, "I'm Tiff and before we start the bonding process, I need to wash my face and go to the bathroom. Where is it? I don't see another door in here."

"Yeah," added the girl with shiny black hair, "I GGP too."

The girl with the brown hair tucked up into a baseball cap giggled and said, "You have to GG, what?"

"GGP," explained the girl. "Gotta go pee."

Lily ignored the potty talk and pointed to a white sink sticking out of the wall. "As you can see, you can wash your hands and face here. If you need to use the toilet, you need to walk outside to the outhouse."

"The what house?" Tiff asked looking confused.

"The out-house!" the girl in the baseball cap blurted out. "It's that wooden shack out back where spiders live."

Tiff looked horrified and shrunk back into her bed.

"You're JK, about using this outside toilet, right?" the girl with the black hair asked.

"No, I am not kidding," said Lily who fully understood text message codes from her own constant use of a cell phone. "The toilet is in that building which is called an outhouse. Inside you will find a toilet seat and toilet paper just like at home. You will also take your showers in another building down the trail that we call the shower stall. But for now, I will show you the outhouse and then...."

"Oh, no," interrupted Tiff. "I refuse to use that thing."

"And I refuse to stay here without an outlet next to my bed for my laptop," said the other girl.

"And I refuse to stay in this cabin with a bunch of whiny wimps," declared the girl in the baseball cap.

Lily took a deep breath and exhaled slowly. Her heart was beating a mile a minute so she tried to focus on the breathing techniques she used in Yoga.

"Excuse me!" Tiffany interrupted Lily's thoughts. "I really need to go to the bathroom. And I mean a real bathroom, not some hole in the ground."

Lily smiled and said sweetly, "I'm sorry, but we all use the same bathroom around here, which is the one outside. Both of you can come with me and I'll show you where it is."

"Fine," said Tiff with a huff, "but I know this is going to be super gross."

The three rounded the corner of the cabin and trudged towards the wooden outhouse. The smell of the outhouse came upon them quickly. Lily went on ahead and opened the door. Sunlight from a tiny window lit up the shiny white toilet seat surrounded by wood. A single roll of white toilet paper sat on the floor.

Tiff moaned as she stepped up next to Lily holding her nose.

"Go ahead," encouraged Lily. "The quicker you go, the sooner you will be done."

Tiff stepped in and gasped as she looked down the hole and saw lumps of used toilet paper swirling around in blue water.

"This is the grossest, nastiest experience of my entire life!" Tiff yelled as Lily closed the door.

As they waited, Lily turned to the other girl and asked, "What is your name?"

"Hanna."

"Have you ever been to camp before?"

"Negative," she replied. "And I certainly have never been forced to use such an unsanitary and primitive toilet before."

Great, thought Lily. I have two very inexperienced, and very upset, campers in my cabin.

The wooden door suddenly swung open. Tiff slammed it behind her and glared at Lily. "That experience is going to emotionally scar me for life!" She then pushed past Lily and started running back up the trail.

"Do you need me to stay here with you?" Lily asked Hanna.

"Nah," Hanna said. "I can handle it. It's NBD."

Lily ran all the way back to the cabin and opened the door. Tiff was crying and trying to pull her trunk out the door.

"I am calling William and telling him to turn around and take me home immediately!" Tiff cried tearfully.

"That's not possible," Lily said gently. "He can't pick you up without your parent's written permission and I believe your parents are in Europe so...."

"I know where my parents are!" cried Tiff. "If he won't come then I will just run away!"

Lily watched as Tiff continued to pull at the heavy trunk. What should she say to calm her down? Maybe she should give up on being a counselor and resign now before things got even worse!

# The Favorites

## KAT

The blonde girl was cracking her up! Kat could not resist teasing this prissy princess of a girl.

"How are you going to run away if you can't even pick up your own trunk?" Kat asked as she sat on her bunk and watched Tiff try to budge the heavy trunk out from under the bed.

She then continued the teasing by adding, "Don't forget that there are lots of spiders in the woods. And, you will definitely have to pee in a hole in the ground in the woods if you go out there!" Kat started laughing so hard she had to hold her stomach as she tried to catch her breath.

"This is not funny," Lily said to Kat. "Not all campers are experienced like you so let's try to be a little nicer and make others feel at home, okay?"

The cabin door opened and the girl with black hair walked back in and glanced at Tiff. Kat saw her smirk and laugh a little as she climbed back into the bunk.

"I see you survived the outhouse," Kat said to her.

"Yeah," replied the girl with the black hair, "It was gross but it's not something to cry about."

Kat looked back towards the prissy girl who was still crying as she struggled to move her trunk. Kat started laughing again but then saw the counselor glaring at her.

"Sorry," said Kat as tried to suppress a giggle. "But she cracks me up! This is better than watching TV!"

"Don't remind me," said the girl with the black hair. "How am I going to survive the summer without TV?"

"I know," agreed Kat. "My favorite show is *Hannah Montana*. I never miss that show!"

"I love that show, too!" exclaimed Hanna.

"I have an idea!" Lily said. "Let's all tell each other a few of our favorite things! We can share our favorite TV show, favorite animal, favorite school subject, favorite color and our favorite food! And make sure you say your name first so we can get to know each other."

"That sounds like fun," said Kat. "Can I go first?"

"Sure," said Lily, looking relieved.

"Okay! My name is Katherine but everyone calls me Kat. I'm from Greenville, South Carolina. You already know that my all time favorite show is *Hannah Montana*. My favorite animal is a tiger, the mascot for Clemson, my favorite college football team! I love the color orange and my favorite school subject is P.E. and my favorite food is barbeque ribs with lots of sauce."

Kat noticed that the blonde girl had finally given up on the trunk and was sitting up wiping the tears off her face. She felt a little bad that she had teased her so much so she asked, "Hey, do you want to go next?"

## TIFF

What Tiff wanted more than anything, was to go home and leave this place forever. But, she also knew that Lily was right. She was stuck here so she might as well make the best of it.

She sighed and replied, "My name is Tiffany but my nickname is Tiff. I'm from Savannah, Georgia. My favorite show is *The Suite Life of Zack and Cody*. I would love to be like that girl named London who lives in the fancy hotel that her dad owns. Not in this gross place."

"What is your favorite animal?" asked Lily.

Tiff was still mad at Lily but she answered, "I love dogs, especially poodles. My aunt has a beautiful white teacup poodle named Snowflake. I've always wanted a puppy. I would buy it a pretty collar with rhinestones with a matching leash."

"Let me guess," Kat said sarcastically. "Your favorite color is pink and you love things that are soft and fluffy."

"Well, yeah," Tiff replied, a little confused, "Do you have a problem with that?"

Kat snorted and Tiff scowled right at Kat. They both continued to glare at each other until Lily interrupted the staring contest and asked, "Tiff, what is your favorite food?"

Tiff glared a few seconds longer at Kat and then turned to Lily and replied, "I love lobster with lots of melted butter. And my favorite period at school is lunch since that is the only time I get to sit and talk to all my friends."

"Lunch is not a class," said the girl with the black hair. "Pick a real subject where you get an actual grade."

"Okay," shrugged Tiff. "I'll pick Art instead because I love to draw."

"Art is an elective," said Hanna.

"So, what's your point?" asked Tiff.

## HANNA.

Hanna could not believe these girls, picking lunch, P.E. and Art as their favorite subjects in school!

"Whatever," she mumbled to herself as she turned her attention to the rest of the group and said, "My name is Hanna and I'm from Atlanta. My favorite show is *Kim Possible*. I love all her gadgets and her cool computer. I need to know where an outlet is in this cabin ASAP so I can plug in my computer. The battery is getting really low."

She climbed down from her bunk and looked under Tiff's bed. "Nope, not one there either." Hanna looked up and stared at Lily, waiting for a reply.

Lily shrugged and said, "Sorry but we don't allow computers in the cabin. But there is a Cyber Corner in the corner of the Dining Hall where you can charge your battery and get access to the Internet."

"Great," Hanna said in a sarcastic tone as she crossed her arms and sat back on the bed. "I am officially cut off from civilization."

Kat leaned towards Hanna and asked, "What's your favorite food? Computer chips?" Kat roared with laughter and rolled back on her bed.

"It's rude to laugh at your own jokes," Hanna said.

"That was a joke?" asked Tiff. "I thought it was just a stupid comment."

Hanna gave Tiff a quick smile and continued, "My favorite food is sushi and my favorite class in school is Technology."

"That's an elective!" Hanna heard Tiff yell.

"Technology is the foundation of everything we do," Hanna replied. "So I don't consider it an elective. I'll probably forget everything I've learned living in these primitive accommodations. I'm going to be BOOMS here."

"Booms?" asked Kat. "Why do you use those weird words?"

Hanna shrugged and replied, "I use them all the time when I send a text or an instant message so I end up using them when I talk. When I say BOOMS it means I am *bored out of my skull.*"

"When you say *primitive accommodations*," asked Tiff, "do you mean *gross camp?*"

Hanna had to laugh. "Yeah," she replied, "same thing."

## LILY

Lily was starting to relax now that some of the girls were at least talking to each other. She could tell that the last girl with the red hair didn't want to talk yet so she decided to go next.

"My name is Lily and I'm from Charlotte, North Carolina, which isn't too far from here. I love *American Idol,* my favorite class is History, and I love Angel Food cake with strawberries and whipped cream. My favorite color is blue and I love this camp. I have been coming here every summer for the past six years! Even though you might think right now that it is primitive and gross, I know you will end up having a lot of fun."

Lily looked at each of the girls and said in a sincere voice, "Just give it a chance, okay?"

Lily continued to look around carefully at each of the girls. Kat would be fine; she seemed like an experienced camper. Tiff and Hanna might have a tough time adjusting without their normal luxuries at home. Lily was worried most about the shy girl. She looked over and saw that she was still sitting on the bed staring at the ground curling a strand of hair with one finger. Would she ever come out of her shell?

## AMY

Amy didn't notice that all eyes were on her since her thoughts were on Rascal. What was she thinking when she hid Rascal in her backpack? How was she going to hide him from her cabin mates? How would she take him out to play? What would she feed him? Amy's heart sank as she thought of how much Rascal must be missing his cage right now.

"Are you okay?" Lily interrupted Amy's thoughts. "You look so sad and worried."

"Oh, I'm fine," Amy mumbled softly. "I'm just a little homesick. I was thinking of how much I … miss my mom."

"I understand," Lily said. "I used to miss my family a lot when I first started coming to camp. Soon you will be having so much fun you won't be homesick at all. I promise."

Lily then added, "If you don't want to take your turn you don't have to. We can wait."

Amy sat up straight and replied shyly, "No, that's okay." She took a deep breath and said, "My name is Amy and I live with my mom in Birmingham, Alabama. I love any show on *Animal Planet*. I love all animals and the color green. My favorite subject is English and I love spaghetti with marinara sauce."

"Spaghetti?" exclaimed Kat as she jumped up and headed towards the door. "That's what I smell! Follow me to the Dining Hall ... I know the way!"

# THE FOOD FIGHT

## AMY

Amy was relieved that the smell of spaghetti had interrupted her time to talk. She hated talking in front of people. She shuffled slowly behind the group as they entered the Dining Hall.

The room was huge! There were ten long wooden tables with benches. Each bench sat at least twenty campers. Several large wooden paddle fans clicked nosily above and the huge screen windows created a strong breeze across the large hall. Along one wall was the serving line where the assistant counselors dished out servings of spaghetti. Amy spotted a separate self-serve bar for salads and another bar for ice cream sundaes.

Amy headed to the line behind Kat and picked up her tray. She could see Hanna heading in the other direction and Tiff checking out the sundae bar. Even an ice cream sundae couldn't cheer her up because she knew she would never fit in here. Her cabin mates were so different from her. Tiff was so pretty, Hanna seemed super smart and Kat was probably good at sports. Amy knew that she was just plain looking, she made average grades at school and she couldn't throw or catch a ball.

But she remembered how her dad would tell her how special she was. He said she reminded him of an angel, with her curly red hair and fair complexion. He said she was an angel with a heart of gold and that a good heart was the most important thing to have. Amy believed everything her dad had told her, but now she was beginning to think that being beautiful, smart and athletic were more important!

Amy turned her thoughts back to Rascal. She needed to get him some food and let him out of her backpack to get some fresh air. She was also worried about Rascal being nocturnal which meant he slept most of the day and played at night. How was she going to keep him quiet so that the other girls didn't hear him?

Amy spied the assortment of raw vegetables on the salad bar and headed over to load up on carrots and lettuce for Rascal. Then, behind the salad bar, she saw a small crate propped against the wall. This would make a great house for Rascal! She would try to come back here later and get it when no one was looking.

## TIFF

"Yum," said Tiff, "look at all the ice cream!"

Tiff could hear her mother's voice in her head telling her that she already had enough sugar today when she felt someone bump into her shoulder. She glanced back to see a blob of chocolate sauce on her new Lily Pulitzer dress.

"Hey!" she yelled, "someone got chocolate on my new dress!"

Tiff looked around to determine who the culprit was, but everyone around her scurried away.

Fuming, she grabbed a napkin and tried to dab off the sauce when she noticed Kat giggling nearby. Tiff didn't waste any time as she grabbed a can of whipped cream, ran up to Kat, and sprayed the entire contents of whipped cream on her shocked face.

There, she said triumphantly to herself as she turned and walked away. That will teach that loud-mouthed tomboy who the boss was around here.

## KAT

Kat stood there with whipped cream sliding down her face. As she looked around for a napkin to wipe off the white goo, she spotted a bowl of red Jell-O. Kat grabbed the bowl and bolted towards Tiff who was walking quickly towards the other side of the Dining Hall. She could see her blonde hair bobbing through the crowd.

"You're not going to get away from me," Kat huffed under her breath. She quickly caught up with Tiff, grabbed her arm and pulled her around to face her.

"Let go of me!" Tiff yelled. "You …"

Kat didn't wait for Tiff to finish. She quickly dumped the entire bowl of Jell-O on Tiff's perfect blonde head. Tiff gasped and wiped the red Jell-O from her eyes. Kat stood back and grinned at her in triumph when Tiff reached over to the table next to her, grabbed a handful of some random girl's spaghetti and smeared it into Kat's face.

Kat gasped in shock. Before she could react, she heard someone yell, "Food Fight!"

The entire Dining Hall erupted into a flurry of food. Spaghetti noodles and meatballs whipped through the air. Campers tossed lettuce into the air like confetti. Some kids scrambled under their table for safety while other stood on their chairs and launched food at every moving target.

Kat was caught up in the excitement. She grabbed a bowl of peas and, before Tiff could duck, bombarded her with mushy green bullets.

A loud whistle shrilled through the large room and the voice of the Camp Director, Mr. Donovan boomed over a microphone, "Stop this nonsense immediately and report to your cabin!"

## HANNA

Hanna was fuming as she grabbed a napkin to wipe a meatball from laptop case. She had found the Cyber Corner and was sitting there minding her own business when a huge meatball dripping with tomato sauce came flying through the air and landed right on Hello Kitty's face!

"This is so gross!" Hanna moaned as she reached for another napkin. How could her parents send her to such an uncivilized place?

Food was everywhere—on the floor, on the chairs and even on top of the heads of some campers! Boy, Hanna said to herself, I feel sorry for whoever has to clean up this mess! She also felt sorry for herself. All she had wanted to do was spend a few minutes on her laptop to cruise her favorite web sites. Instead, she was the innocent victim of a food fight!

Hanna pulled the strap of her laptop case over her shoulder and walked slowly towards Lily, who was waving at her from the corner of the Dining Hall. She stepped carefully over piles of spaghetti and mashed peas. How was she ever going to last two whole weeks in this disgusting place?

# The Punishment

## LILY

Lily could not believe it. She stepped away from her girls for just a few minutes to say hi to some of her fellow counselors and they start a food fight! She knew that Mr. Donovan would call her into his office and talk to her about the importance of watching her campers at all times. He might even demote her to assistant counselor!

"I can't believe this," she moaned to herself as she walked slowly behind her campers. Kat was leading the pack, walking quickly up the path while she tucked her sticky hair into her baseball cap. Hanna was still fuming as she continued to wipe the front of her laptop case with a wet napkin as she walked behind Kat. Amy trotted behind with her arms wrapped around her backpack that she held closely to her chest. Tiff walked quietly behind the other girls as she pulled peas and clumps of Jell-O out of her hair.

As they reached the cabin, Kat turned and asked, "So, what are we going to do now? I never got to eat, so I'm still hungry."

"Just get inside," said Lily, trying to control her temper. "After the scene you just caused I doubt any of us will get to eat tonight."

"What?" asked Tiff, "No dinner? That's child abuse or neglect or something like that. You have to feed us—it's the law!"

Lily felt exhausted. Her first day as a counselor was a disaster.

"Just get inside," she repeated trying to stay calm. "I am sure we will get something to eat but it won't be spaghetti served in the Dining Hall thanks to you and your friends ..."

"Friends?" Kat said as she glared at Tiff. "Princess here is NOT my friend."

"You're right about that!" Tiff said as she stomped into the cabin.

Lily followed the girls and watched as Hanna went straight to the sink to get more water and a clean paper towel. Tiff and Kat stood in the middle of room and glared at each other.

Tiff suddenly turned to Lily and asked, "Where's the dressing room? I need to take this dress off and send it to the dry cleaners."

## KAT

When Tiff asked about the dry cleaners, Kat cracked up laughing. She laughed even harder when she saw that Lily was trying her best not to laugh also. Kat kept laughing as she watched Lily take a deep breath and explain to Tiff that there was not a dressing room in the cabin and no dry cleaner at the camp.

As Tiff pouted, Kat stopped laughing and said to Lily, "I can't believe Princess here dumped food all over my hair."

"Well, you started it!" Tiff yelled at her.

"I did not!" Kat yelled back. "You just came up and sprayed whipped cream in my face for no reason!"

"You smeared chocolate on my new dress!"

"It wasn't me!" Kat yelled back. "And besides, only an idiot wears a new dress to camp!"

"Both of you participated in the food fight so both of you are at fault," Lily explained, "and both of you will need to take a shower tonight."

Kat had already taken a shower this morning before she left for camp. She really didn't want to have to take two showers in one day but her hair was sticky and even her baseball cap couldn't hide the whipped cream and spaghetti noodles.

The door suddenly swung open and in came two assistant counselors, each one carrying the end of an ice chest. They dumped it in the middle of the cabin and said, "Everyone has to stay in their cabin for dinner. Here are some drinks. Pizza will be here in about thirty minutes."

As they turned to leave one said, "Oh yeah, the marshmallow roast and sing-a-long has been cancelled tonight. Everyone has to stay in their cabin with lights out at 9:00 p.m. sharp."

"Well," said Lily as she opened the ice chest to reveal bottled water and soft drinks on ice, "that's our punishment. There will be no singing around the campfire tonight. You will have to wait for the next campfire which is not until the end of the week."

As the girls groaned in unison, Lily turned back to Tiff and Kat and said, "Grab your towels, clean clothes and your shower caddy. I'll walk with you to the shower stall."

She then turned to Amy and Hanna and said, "We should be back before the pizza arrives but if it comes before we get back you can go ahead and start eating."

## TIFF

Tiff stood in the middle of the cabin and looked around for her shower caddy. I might as well be in prison, she thought to herself as she peeked under her bunk bed. This place has stripped me of all my dignity and now I have to eat and sleep with a juvenile delinquent!

Tiff pulled out her shower caddy and followed Lily and Kat out of the cabin. She held her caddy in one hand and had her towel and clothes over her shoulder. She really missed William right now. If he were here, he would be carrying all this stuff for her!

She glanced down at her caddy that was a plastic bucket with compartments for her shampoo, body soap, flip-flops, etc. Tiff had imagined using the caddy in a nice clean shower in her cabin! She had no idea that she would have to carry it through the woods to some stupid shower stall!

Tiff followed Kat and Lily as they quickly made their way down the trail. As they turned a corner, Tiff looked ahead and saw a square gray building sitting out in a small clearing—right in the middle of nowhere.

"That's it?" she said as she stopped in her tracks. "That's where the showers are?"

"Yes," Lily said. "I'll go in with you and show you how to turn on the water. The water is pretty cold so don't plan on staying in there very long."

"A cold shower?" exclaimed Tiff. "I'm getting punished twice in one night!"

Tiff stood glued to the ground as she watched Kat go into the building. A few seconds later, she heard water running and Kat whistling a tune. Great, she mumbled to herself, leave it to that tomboy to make this dreadful experience seem fun.

"Come on," Lily said as opened the door for Tiff. The inside looked just like the outside, with gray concrete blocks on the walls. The ceiling had wood planks and a few yellow light bulbs cast an eerie glow in the stark room. On the left, wooden benches lined the walls with hooks above. On the right wall there several sinks and mirrors. Straight ahead on the back wall, Tiff saw a row of six showers. There were no doors, just flimsy white plastic shower curtains.

Lily went up to a shower and pulled back the curtain. "Here, I'll go ahead and turn on the water for you so it will start warming up a little."

Tiff heard Kat continue to whistle a happy tune. I can do this, Tiff told herself. I am just as tough as she is.

As Lily stepped out, Tiff stepped in and yanked the curtain closed. There was a small area outside of the shower with a bench and a hook to hang her towel and another for her clothes. Tiff leaned into the shower and inspected the floor for bugs. She then looked up and cringed when she saw spider webs on the ceiling.

"Oh, don't forget to wear your flip-flops in the shower," Lily yelled through the curtain. "You don't want to get a fungus."

Just great, thought Tiff, I'll probably get some disease and my toes will rot off! She had wondered why flip-flops were included in the list with the shower caddy. Tiff kept on her flip-flops and took off her sticky clothes. She carefully stepped into the shower and began lathering her hair when she felt something tickling her toes. Looking down, she saw a huge green lizard enjoying the shower with her!

"Eww!" she yelled as she jumped out of the shower and hugged her towel around her.

"What's wrong?" she heard Lily ask through the curtain.

"A huge lizard was crawling on my foot!"

"It won't hurt you," said Lily. "It just likes the water. It's probably more scared of you than you are of it."

I doubt that, Tiff said to herself as she peeked back into the shower. The lizard was gone. Where was it? She looked up and down the walls of the shower but didn't see anything but old gray tiles. Tiff heard Kat turn off her shower. Kat was already finished with her shower! Tiff panicked. She needed to hurry and not worry about this stupid lizard. She stepped back into the shower and starting washing as quickly as she could.

"Hurry up, princess," she heard Kat yell. "If we wait any longer, the bats will be out flying around and one might land in your hair."

Tiff froze—first an outhouse, then a cold shower with a slimy lizard, and now bats? Could things get any worse?

## HANNA

Hanna and Amy sat in awkward silence. Hanna saw that Amy had her journal in her lap and was writing something down. Hanna wondered what she was writing.

Amy seemed very shy, and a little sad, thought Hanna. Maybe she should make an effort to talk to her about something, anything to break the uncomfortable silence in the room.

After a few more minutes of silence Hanna said, "I wonder what kind of pizza they are bringing us."

Amy looked up and replied, "I hope they have plain cheese pizza. I don't eat pepperoni."

"I hate pepperoni, too! Actually, I don't eat any meat, just fish. I love sushi."

"I'm a vegetarian," said Amy. "The thought of eating anything that has a face makes me nauseous."

"I guess you will just be eating from the salad bar at this camp," said Hanna, "and the ice cream bar!"

Amy nodded and smiled a little.

Boy, she's a hard one to get to know, Hanna thought to herself. At least the other two girls were entertaining to watch. This one was just boring with a capital B!.

Hanna sighed in relief as Lily came through the door with Tiff and Kat close behind. Both girls had their hair wrapped in a towel. As they headed towards their bunks, the door opened again and in came a counselor carrying several boxes of pizza.

"Enjoy!" she said as she placed the pizza on the table and quickly left the room.

"Perfect timing!" said Lily as she opened the boxes.

Hanna watched as Kat and Tiff both ran to the box that smelled like pepperoni and sausage. Well, she thought, at least they both have one thing in common.

Hanna opened the next box and said to Amy, who was still sitting quietly on her bunk. "This one is cheese. Here, take a piece."

"Don't you guys want some of this one?" Kat asked with her mouth full. "The pepperoni is great!"

"No thanks. We don't meat."

"Oh, so you're veterinarian," exclaimed Tiff.

Hanna cracked up laughing as Tiff and Kat both looked a bit confused.

"No," Amy said calmly. "A veterinarian is what my Mom is, which means she takes care of animals, like a doctor. I am a vegetarian which means I don't eat animals."

"Oh," said Tiff as she shrugged her shoulders. "Sounds almost like the same thing to me. You both save animals, right?'

"Right," said Amy with a smile. "I guess it is kind of the same thing."

"So, what are we going to do tonight, now that we are stuck inside this cabin?" Hanna asked.

"We can turn off the light and tell ghost stories," Tiff said. "I learned some really scary stories from some girls when I stayed over-night in Atlanta for the Little Miss Georgia Pageant."

Hanna crinkled up her nose and asked, "You were in a beauty pageant in Atlanta?"

Tiff tossed her hair and said proudly, "Yes, and I came in second place. Maybe you saw me on TV on the news."

"I seriously doubt you were on the news in Atlanta. They only report *real* news. Not some story about girls parading around in bathing suits," Hanna scoffed.

Kat suddenly jumped up, yanked the towel off her head and flipped her hair around while she pranced around the cabin with her hands on her hips singing, "Here, she is....Miss Ameri-dork ..."

"Ameri dork.... that's a good one!" Hanna said as she broke out in laughter while Kat continued to imitate a beauty queen walking down the runway.

"C'mon girls," Lily said. "Don't make fun of Tiff's accomplishments. Competing in a beauty pageant is hard work."

"How do you know?" Hanna asked Lily. "Were you a beauty queen, too?"

"No," explained Lily, "but I've been in a lot of dance competitions so I know the level of dedication and hard work it takes to memorize a routine and perform on stage."

Tiff added, "You're just jealous because you probably haven't won any awards before."

Kat plopped down next to Hanna and the room was quiet for a moment until Hanna decided to speak up.

"Actually, I have won some awards," replied Hanna. "But my parents don't like for me to boast about my accomplishments."

"Oh, go ahead and boast," said Kat sarcastically. "We won't tell them."

Hanna looked around and saw everyone, even her counselor, staring at her with encouragement.

"Fine," said Hanna, "Let's see, I've won the state spelling bee every year for the last three years, my science project came in first at the county science fair last year, and my team was first in Math Olympics."

Tiff looked stunned and sat back down on her bed.

Kat looked surprised too and said, "Wow, the only thing I've won is some dinky trophies with my soccer and softball team."

Tiff then said to Hanna, "If you are such a brain what are you doing at a camp like this?"

Hanna replied, "I didn't want to come here. This camp is definitely NFM. I wanted to be at the NASA space camp or a computer camp but my parents said I needed 'fresh air and sunshine' so here I am, BOOMS and stuck here in the middle of nowhere...."

## AMY

Amy surprised everyone by interrupting and saying, "I know how you feel. I was hoping to volunteer at the Humane Society this summer but my mom said I needed fresh air and new friends too, so here I am."

Amy hated being the center of attention. But now everyone was looking right her and she cringed when Tiff asked her, "So, what awards have you won, Amy?"

"I won the school Citizenship Award," Amy said softly as she clutched her blanket to her chest and looked at the floor.

"The city-what?" asked Kat.

"The Citizenship Award," Hanna answered for Amy. "Our school has that award. It goes to the student who is the best citizen. You know ... the most polite and helpful."

"Amy," Lily said as she joined the conversation, "that is a wonderful accomplishment!"

Lily continued as she looked directly at Tiff and Kat, "All of us should try to be a great citizen. You know, following rules, respecting other people's property ..."

Amy was relieved that everyone was now looking at Tiff and Kat but that didn't last long as Hanna turned to Amy and said sincerely, "That's great, Amy. You really should be very proud of yourself."

Amy smiled meekly and shrugged her shoulders. She was proud that she won that award. She always tried to help others, including animals.

Her thoughts turned back to her dilemma with Rascal. She wished she could trust her cabin mates and ask for their help with Rascal. She needed to get that crate so that Rascal could get out of the backpack.

An idea came to her. "After we finish eating, why don't we help clean up the mess in the Dining Hall?"

"Now you're taking this best citizen stuff too far," said Tiff. "I'm not cleaning up that mess."

"But you started it," said Hanna. "You should help clean it up."

"I did not start it!" yelled Tiff, "Someone smeared chocolate on...."

"Amy and Hanna are both right," interrupted Lily. "We should volunteer to help clean. We are a team so that means that everyone here will help."

Groans filled the cabin and Hanna exclaimed, "That's not fair! I was just an innocent bystander!"

"Lily, do we really have to help clean up?" Tiff asked sweetly, "I'm sure the money our parents paid for this camp covers the cost of cleaning up our messes."

"It's not about the money," Lily explained carefully. "It's about being responsible for your actions."

Amy gulped down her food as fast as she could. As her cabin mates sulked and slowly ate their pizza, she hustled around the cabin picking up empty cans and pizza boxes.

"Sit down and relax," Lily told her. "We don't need to hurry."

"I know," said Amy, trying to look calm. "I'm just in a hurry to go help clean the Dining Hall."

"Are you for real?" Kat asked through a mouthful of cheese. "You're in a hurry to clean?"

Amy ignored Kat's remark and turned directly to Lily. "Since I'm done eating, would it be okay with you if I went ahead to the Dining Hall?"

"Sure," Lily replied, "We should be there in about ten minutes."

"Thanks!" Amy said over her shoulder as she darted out the door.

As the door slammed shut behind her, she heard Hanna say, "Something is up with that girl."

Amy didn't wait around to hear what else they would say about her. These girls were not her friends so she did not care what they thought of her. Rascal was her best friend and he was all that mattered to her right now.

# THE CLEAN UP

## AMY

Amy reached the Dining Hall and slipped in the side door. Several assistant counselors were already mopping the floor and complaining about the campers. Amy eyed the salad bar. The food was gone and it stood there empty. She tiptoed nervously to the bar and peered over the top, relieved to see the small crate still propped against the wall. Amy slid behind the bar and grabbed the crate. It was perfect for Rascal. All she needed was to put some sort of lid on top.

"Hey," a voice yelled. "What are you doing over there? You're supposed to be in your cabin!"

Amy froze and a tear started to slide down her cheek. Just then, a familiar voice filled the empty Dining Hall. "It's okay, she's with me."

Lily appeared through the side door and waved at the counselors. "She's one of my campers and she volunteered to help clean up. The rest of my cabin will be here in a few minutes, so save some work for them!"

"You betcha!" smiled one of the counselors as they went back to their mopping. "There's plenty of mess here for everyone!"

Lily walked over to Amy. As she got closer, she saw the tears and the crate and said softly, "Do you want to tell me what is going on?"

Amy squeezed her eyes shut trying to keep more tears from spilling down her face. Why did she sneak in Rascal? What would they do with him if they found out? What will her mom do when she found out? She burst out in tears and covered her face with the small crate.

Lily put her arm around her shoulders and walked her to one of the over stuffed chairs in the Cyber Corner. "Here," she said gently, "Sit here while I get you a napkin and a glass of water. Then you can tell me what's up."

## LILY

Lily was relieved that Amy had finally shared her secret with her. She was also nervous about the conversation she would need to have with Mr. Donovan. She knew about the rule on pets but how could she tell Amy she couldn't keep her gerbil? The girl was so lonely and she poured her heart out to Lily. She was still depressed about losing her father and it seemed like her mom worked a lot so her only company was her pets and Rascal was her favorite.

Some kids bring a favorite teddy bear to camp. Amy brings a gerbil—what's the big deal? "A huge deal," Lily muttered aloud to herself. "First a food fight, and now a stowaway gerbil."

Well, she might as well get it over with and head over the director's cabin she told herself. She heard the door open and saw Hanna coming into the Dining Hall.

"Hey," she yelled across the room. "I need to go to the director's cabin for a few minutes. You can start wiping down the tables with Amy. When Tiff and Kat show up, tell them to start mopping the floors. I'll be back in a few minutes."

## HANNA

Hanna could tell Amy was upset about something. Her eyes were all red and swollen from crying and she was making an effort to avoid eye contact with Hanna. Hanna didn't ask what was wrong; she didn't like to get involved in other people's personal business.

Besides, she had enough worry about, being stuck at this camp. This was going to be the worst summer ever. She had no electrical outlet for her laptop, stains on her laptop case, and now she had to help clean up a huge mess that she didn't even make.

Hanna grabbed a sponge and thought about Tiff and Kat who were still goofing off in the cabin. Tiff was such a spoiled princess. However, she and Tiff did have one thing in common—they both appreciated the finer things in life. Not like Kat and Amy who actually seemed to enjoy being in the wilderness!

Hanna thought about what she would be doing if she were at home. Most likely, she would be in her room downloading songs on her iPod and checking out new games on the Internet. She would crank up her air conditioner so it was nice and cool in her room and her Mom would make her a yogurt smoothie with fresh strawberries and bananas. She would also talk online to her favorite friend, Alex.

Alex really seemed to understand Hanna. She felt like she knew more about him than any of the kids in her school. She wished she could tell someone about Alex but she didn't dare. Everyone would assume he was some sort of cyber creep or something. Hanna felt bad not telling her parents but if they knew she was talking online with a "stranger" they would take away her laptop! Hanna wasn't going to let anyone know about Alex. It was her secret.

Might as well get this over with, Hanna thought as sprayed the table and began wiping. At least she was out of that stuffy cabin and might have time to chat with Alex in the Cyber Corner.

## KAT

Kat dumped her plate into the trashcan and headed for the cabin door.

"Wait!" Tiff said, "… can you wait a second so we can walk together?"

"You're not scared to be outside in the dark," Kat teased. "Are you?"

"Okay, I admit that this place gives me the creeps," confessed Tiff. "What is that strange noise outside?"

"Crickets," said Kat. "They are supposed to bring you good luck."

"Yeah, well I am definitely going to need a lot of luck to survive this place."

"Oh, you're going to need more than luck," laughed Kat. "You're going to need a maid, a butler, and a private cook!"

"And don't forget my hairdresser," Tiff added as she shook her hair out from under her towel, "Or I might have to borrow your ugly baseball cap to hide my hair!"

Kat laughed at the thought of Tiff with her hair crammed into a baseball cap. She had never been around a prissy girl like this before. She hung out mostly with her three brothers. They were all rough, tough and teased Kat all day. No one got upset—it was just part of the fun!

"C'mon," Kat said. "I'll make sure you get to the Dining Hall safely. I wouldn't want you to get attacked by a lizard or something."

"Gee, thanks," Tiff said as she followed Kat out of the cabin.

The leaves crunched under their feet as they walked towards the Dining Hall. The sun was starting to go down and the tall trees cast shadows on the trail. Kat heard crickets and an owl hooting in the distance and noticed Tiff glance nervously towards the woods. Kat smiled and began thinking about a surprise she would have for the princess later tonight.

When they reached the Dining Hall, Kat flung open the door and announced, "We're here! Put us to work!"

"Gladly," said Hanna as she glared at both of them. "Lily said for you both to grab a mop and clean the floor."

"Mopping?" yelled Kat. "I love to mop!"

## TIFF

Tiff was actually having fun sloshing the bubbly water on the floor and mopping it up. At first, Tiff was upset that she had to mop. After watching Kat have fun sliding on the floor with her bare feet, Tiff tried it and soon they were both laughing and singing crazy songs while they mopped.

Even though she was having fun, Tiff was still mad at Kat. She might be having fun with her now but she still thought Kat was mean and she certainly didn't trust her. Tiff knew she could never be friends with someone as weird as Kat, with her tomboy clothes and constant wad of gum in her mouth.

"Hey," Tiff yelled over to Kat. "We missed a spot over here."

Tiff dunked her mop into the bucket and sloshed water on the floor under the table. Kat slid over next to her and helped mop up the sticky spaghetti sauce.

Tiff looked over at the two other girls and wondered if she would become friends with them. Amy was so shy and Tiff didn't think she could ever be friends with someone who was so serious and moody. Hanna seemed nice at first but then she was so mean when she found out that Tiff was in a beauty pageant! What was Hanna's problem? Pageants were fun, a lot more fun than science fairs and Math Olympics!

Tiff knew that most girls were jealous of her, so she wasn't surprised that her cabin mates didn't like her. After all, she was prettier than they were and she definitely had nicer things than they had. She was shocked when she saw the old clothes girls wore at this camp! This place was a fashion nightmare!

No, Tiff thought to herself, this is not just a fashion nightmare but a total nightmare! Tiff thought of her cousin who had invited her to New York this summer. Instead, her parents made her come to this stupid camp. Now, instead of shopping—she was mopping!

The fun fizzled and Tiff put her mop in the bucket and declared, "I quit."

Just then, the screen door opened and Lily walked in and said, "Great job, girls! I need to talk to Amy for a few minutes so we are heading back to the cabin. You guys put away the mops and spray and head on back to the cabin."

# THE CONFESSION

## AMY

Amy walked behind Lily down the trail towards the cabin with the crate tucked under her arm. She could not believe how nice Lily was about Rascal. Lily told her that Mr. Donovan, the camp director, would call Amy's mom and tell her it was okay for Rascal to stay at camp. Her mom should be arriving home soon and she would panic when she saw that Rascal was not in his cage in the back seat.

Amy could see the cabin up ahead. Tiny moths danced around the small yellow light bulb that glowed above the door. Amy's steps slowed as she thought about what the other girls in the cabin would think of Rascal. Amy had promised Lily that she would tell the others about Rascal as soon as they got back to the cabin. Amy was sure Kat would be okay with it, she was so easy going, but Hanna and Tiff might not like Rascal. Neither one seemed to care about animals very much ... just fancy computers and clothes.

"Come on," Lily said gently as she opened the door of the cabin for Amy.

As Amy stepped into the cabin, she could hear the other girls running behind them down the trail. She went quickly to her backpack and gently took Rascal out, placed him in his new crate and put a towel on top.

As Amy scooted the crate behind her trunk, she heard the door open and cringed as Lily announced, "Amy has something she would like to tell everyone."

Everyone stood in the middle of the cabin and stared at Amy. Amy cleared her throat and said softly, "I broke one of the camp rules."

"You?" exclaimed Kat. "Little goodie two shoes?"

Amy tried to smile as she continued, "Yes, me. I knew the camp had a rule against pets but I snuck one in anyway."

"You brought a dog with you?" Tiff asked excitedly. "Is it a poodle?"

"I didn't bring a dog," Amy explained as she gently lifted Rascal from the crate, "but a gerbil."

Tiff jumped back and squealed, "Eww, gross! You mean a rat!"

"Calm down," Lily said. "He's not a rat, he's a gerbil and I am letting Amy keep him here in our cabin. He can be our mascot!"

"He is so cute!" exclaimed Kat. "Can I hold him?"

Amy was relieved that she was right about Kat. At least one of her cabin mates liked Rascal! She gently handed Rascal to Kat and said, "Sure. You can feed him while I set up his crate in the corner of the room. Here are some carrots."

While Amy made Rascal's new home as comfortable as possible, she noticed Hanna watching Kat and Rascal from her bunk.

"Do you have any pets, Hanna?" Amy asked her.

"No," said Hanna. "My dad is allergic to cats and dogs, so we can't have any pets."

"You can hold him too, if you want," Amy offered.

Kat looked up and said, "Come sit next to me, Hanna. You can help me feed him his carrots."

Amy smiled and relaxed for the first time since she arrived at the camp. She felt tired and couldn't wait to curl up with her blanket and close her eyes. She knew Rascal would be okay and everything would now be all right.

## TIFF

Tiff went to the corner of the cabin to brush her teeth while the others played with the rat. She then turned her back to them as she took off her jeans and polo shirt and slipped her white lacey nightgown over her head. She couldn't believe she had to change clothes in front of these girls and share this one tiny sink. Worse of all, she would have to go outside to use the bathroom in that nasty outhouse and take a shower in a dirty stall!

Lily said she would walk back outside with her with a flashlight to the outhouse but there was no way Tiff was going to venture out to the outhouse in the dark. There could be roaches or snakes in there! Tiff shivered at the thought.

Tiff crawled into her bunk and yelled, "Are we telling ghost stories or playing with rats?"

"It's not a rat," Kat said.

"That's right," explained Amy, "He is in the rodent family but he is a gerbil."

"Whatever," said Tiff. "He looks like a rat to me so I'm going to start by telling a story about a girl who lived in a haunted house with a rat …"

"Well," Lily interrupted, "you guys don't need me anymore so I am going to my cabin. Don't forget that lights need to be out tonight at nine sharp."

As she opened the door, she turned and said over her shoulder, "Good night, sleep tight, don't let the bed bugs bite!"

The door slammed behind her and Tiff jumped out of bed and exclaimed, "Bed bugs?"

"Chill out," said Kat. "She was just kidding."

Tiff took a breath and started to relax back onto her bunk when Hanna spoke up and said, "Actually, there are such things as bed bugs. They can live in mattresses and they're kind of like mites or tiny fleas."

"Oh, that is totally disgusting," said Tiff as she jumped back out of bed again and glared suspiciously at her bed.

"It is gross to know that we might be sleeping with bugs," agreed Hanna, "but it is probably not the most disgusting thing that we will encounter while we are in this dismal place."

Tiff then heard Amy talking but could not hear what she was saying.

"Speak up!" Tiff said to Amy, "I can't hear you. You really need to learn how to project your voice. I can show you some exercises my speech coach taught me. First, you …"

"Put a lid on it," Kat yelled from across the room, "and just let her talk."

Tiff sat down with a huff and all eyes were back on Amy.

Amy sat up straight and tried to talk a little louder, "The worse that could happen to you is that you might wake up with tiny red bumps where the bugs have bitten you. If they do bite you, they can't actually hurt you. At least, not like a spider or something."

"How do you know?" Tiff asked. "Have you ever slept in a bed with bugs?"

"No," Amy admitted shyly. "I just read a lot about bugs and animals and I remember reading about bed mites."

"I told you they were mites," Hanna smirked. "There's nothing we can do about it so we might as well get into bed and see if we wake tomorrow with spots!"

"I hate this place," moaned Tiff as she carefully climbed back into her bed. She then had the horrible realization that she had to go to the bathroom. She would try to get her mind off bugs, rats, and bears by focusing on telling her ghost story. She tossed and turned in her bed until she was cozy and warm under the oversized pink comforter.

"Okay guys," she said as she turned on her trusty pink flashlight, "it's story time! Once upon a time there was a large rat and …"

## HANNA

She missed her bed. She could almost feel little bugs crawling all over her. She longed for her shiny bathroom that was only a few feet from her bed at home.

How would she ever survive is this awful place? She was not going to complain like that beauty queen, Tiff. Sure, she hated this place too but she was smart enough to know that whining didn't help. She would need to use her brain to figure out how to make this place more bearable.

Hanna then remembered that her mom had packed her some lavender oil. The smell of lavender is supposed to help you relax, so her mom had suggested that Hanna sprinkle some on her pillow if she couldn't fall asleep. Hanna knew also that lavender oil was also antiseptic and antibacterial, which meant that bugs would not like the smell!

Hanna climbed from the top bunk and started rummaging through her trunk until she found the small bottle tucked away in the corner. She pulled back her blanket and started sprinkling oil on the sheets.

Tiff stopped her story and hissed, "What are you doing?"

Hanna tried to shield her eyes as Tiff shined the flashlight in her face. "Could you shine that thing somewhere else?"

"Oh, sorry," Tiff said as she put the flashlight down. "What is that stuff?"

"I don't know for sure if it will work, but I am sprinkling lavender oil on my sheets. I am hoping the smell will keep the bed bugs away." Hanna explained.

"Can I try some?" Amy spoke up from the other top bunk.

"Sure," Hanna said as she handed the bottle to Amy. "Just use a couple of drops, it's strong."

She then turned to Tiff who was still staring at her. "You can use some too, if you want," she offered.

"Thanks," Tiff said softly as she took the small bottle and sprinkled her sheets.

Hanna turned to Kat who was watching her carefully.

"Do you want some, too?" she asked.

"No thanks," "said Kat. "I don't want my bed to smell like flowers."

"Yeah, she probably likes her bed to smell nice and sweaty," said Tiff.

## KAT

"Hey, I just took a shower, remember?" said Kat as she sat up and glared at Tiff. "So my bed is definitely not sweaty."

Kat curled up on her bed and pulled the long white t-shirt her oldest brother had given her down over her knees. No ruffles or flannel nightgown for her!

Kat was always the last one to fall asleep, which was a good thing since she had a nice surprise waiting for Miss Priss! Sometimes, Kat had trouble going to sleep or she would wake up in the middle of the night. Her mom thought caffeine was keeping her awake and had banned Kat from drinking soft drinks and was even trying to cut chocolate. Kat loved chocolate! She would rather toss and turn all night and wake up tired than give up her Hershey candy bars!

Kat squished her pillow under her head and started listening to Tiff's ghost story. Kat didn't believe in ghosts and she certainly wasn't scared of the dark so ghost stories never scared her. The story Tiff was telling wasn't scary at all. Kat had heard the same one when she was in Brownies three years ago!

After a few minutes, Kat heard heavy breathing and noticed that both Amy and Hanna were sleeping. Tiff noticed too, because she suddenly said, "Hey, is anyone still awake?"

Kat didn't answer and tried not to move a muscle.

She then heard Tiff whine, "I can't believe they went to sleep!"

Kat listened as Tiff tossed and turned a few times and then finally settled down. Within a few minutes, Kat could hear Tiff softly snoring.

So, the princess snores, Kat said to herself with a smile. She quietly slipped out of her bed onto the bare wooden floor. She then crawled across the floor to Tiff's bed and slid under it on her back.

Kat stayed very still and listened to Tiff snore. Let's see if this scares the little princess, Kat thought to herself. First, she pulled out a handful of gummy worms, which she had snuck out of the Dining Hall from the ice cream bar, and tossed them on the floor next to Tiff's bed. Then, she placed the bottom of her feet under the center of Tiff's mattress.

One, two, three…. Kat pushed with her feet and legs as hard as she could, pushing Tiff up into the air and out of her bed.

Tiff tumbled onto the floor screaming. She scrambled to get up and found her hands and feet on squishy worms. Hopping around, Tiff continued to scream as Hanna and Amy both climbed out of their beds.

Someone switched on the overhead light and Tiff stopped hopping around as she looked down at the gummy worms.

"Way to go," Hanna said to Kat as she helped her out from under the bed.

"Glad you approve," Kat said as she brushed dust bunnies off the back of her legs.

"Guys, that wasn't nice," Amy said as she put her arm around Tiff. "You really scared her."

"Consider it your official welcome to camp," Kat explained to Tiff. "You are no longer a princess but an official camper."

Kat walked to her bunk and climbed into bed as the three girls stood and stared at her. "Good night!" she said as she yawned and rolled over.

"I will get you back," Kat heard Tiff say.

"In your dreams," Kat replied as she rolled over, closed her eyes and fell fast asleep.

# THE BLOB

## KAT

The next morning Kat woke up to the sound of a bell ringing. She quickly jumped up and pulled on her clothes. The others woke up slowly, stretching and yawning as they looked around the cabin. Kat watched in amusement as Tiff climbed out of her bed and examined her arms and legs.

"Looking for bug bites?" Kat asked.

Tiff ignored Kat and turned her back to her as she continued to look at her arms. Fine with me, Kat said to herself. I didn't want to talk to her anyway.

Hanna and Amy both examined their arms and legs, too.

"We're fine," Hanna said. "No bug bites."

The screen door opened and Lily stepped in with a big smile on her face, "Good morning!" she said cheerfully. She was waving a white piece of paper in her hand as she announced, "Here is the schedule of events for today—our cabin gets to go first on the Blob!"

"Awesome!" Kat yelled. "You guys are going to have a blast!"

The other girls remained quiet as they all sat on their beds and looked at Lily.

"The Blob is a lot of fun," confirmed Lily. "Get dressed and let's go have breakfast and then we will head down to the lake. I'll be back in a few minutes to walk down to the Dining Hall with you."

Lily left the cabin and the girls started to scurry around. Kat was impressed that Tiff didn't tell Lily about Kat's surprise last night. Maybe Tiff was cool after all.

True to her word, Lily came back five minutes later and led the four back to the Dining Hall. Kat was on her best behavior as she quickly ate her breakfast and then headed back to the cabin to get ready for the day's events.

Kat put on her bathing suit and sneakers, flung her towel over her shoulder, and ran out of the cabin ahead of the others. She ran quickly down the rocky path towards the huge shimmering lake. She shielded her eyes from the bright sun and could see the Blob floating in the water, bouncing softly in the wake from a passing ski boat. It was like a huge floating trampoline but softer and squishier. It reminded Kat of a big inflatable pillow.

Kat loved the Blob and remembered how much fun it was at her last camp. One person sat on the edge of the Blob while another person jumped off a wooden platform. When the camper jumped off the wooden platform onto the Blob, the camper who was sitting of the edge of the Blob would fly up and out into the water. She felt like a trapeze artist at the circus as she flew through the air!

As Kat rounded the last curve in the path, she skidded into a small beach of soft white sand. She kicked off her sneakers, dropped her towel on the ground, grabbed a lifejacket and ran through the hot sand straight for the water.

The lake was like a mirror with pine trees reflected in the dark blue sparkling water. Kat knew she couldn't go in the water until Lily and the rest of her cabin caught up with her so she walked to the water's edge and watched the school of minnows glistening under the water as they darted around just below the surface.

Kat heard someone panting behind and turned to find Hanna trudging onto the beach. "Wow," Hanna said as she tried to catch her breath. "You sure do run fast."

"Not really," replied Kat. "You guys are just slow. Where are the others?"

"Tiff and Amy aren't thrilled about this activity," explained Hanna. "I think Tiff is afraid she might break a fingernail and I don't know what Amy's issue is."

"Well, they don't know what they're missing!" said Kat. "I want to go in the water now. How far up the path are they?"

"Pretty far, but Lily said if the lifeguard was here then we could go ahead and get in the water."

Kat pointed to a cute blonde teenager guy sitting in a lifeguard stand. Hanna gave Kat a nod and they both jumped into the cold water and started swimming towards the wooden platform.

"You're a pretty good swimmer," Kat said with surprise as they pulled themselves up the ladder and plopped down on the warm platform.

"My mom made me take swimming lessons when I was little since I refused to do any other type of sport," explained Hanna. "She also tried to get me to take ballet lessons but I refused to wear the tights so she gave up on that, too!"

"Me, too!" laughed Kat. "I have three older brothers and my mom was so excited to have a little girl she put me into ballet classes. I hated those tights. I would even sit down in the middle of class and try to yank them off!"

They both laughed as they stood up and checked out the Blob.

"It looks a little scary," said Hanna hesitantly.

"Trust me, it is so much fun." Kat said. "You can watch me first."

## HANNA

Hanna watched as Kat walked across the Blob and sat down on the edge facing the water. Kat turned and waved to Hanna as another camper climbed onto the platform and prepared to jump onto the Blob.

"Are you ready?" the camper asked.

"Ready," said Kat.

The other camper jumped and landed in the middle of the Blob. Hanna gasped as she saw Kat go straight up into the air and land about ten feet out into the water.

Kat's head bobbed out of the water and she yelled, "That was awesome!"

Hanna felt her stomach quivering and her heart pounding as she watched Kat climb back onto the platform. She really wanted to do this but she was not a risk taker. She always liked to play it safe and approached every challenge in a practical and logical manner.

There was nothing practical about this, but it looked like so much fun. Isn't that why she came to this camp, to be outside and have fun? By the time Kat reached her, Hanna had made up her mind.

"So...." Kat stood dripping in front of Hanna with her eyebrows raised.

"Let's do this," Hanna said.

"Now it's a little wobbly when you walk on the Blob," explained Kat. "It's kind of like being on a moonwalk. Just try to keep your balance as you walk to the edge and sit down."

Hanna was too scared to talk so she just nodded and climbed down from the platform onto the Blob. She couldn't believe she was actually going to do this! She walked carefully to the edge and sat down. She took a deep breath, then turned and gave Kat thumbs up.

Hanna put her hands down on the squishy plastic and tried to brace herself. Before she knew it, she was up in the air! She felt weightless as she flew higher and higher. She then felt herself going straight down towards the water. She didn't even have time to hold her nose when she plunged into the deep water. The water was cold and dark but Hanna could see the sunlight twinkling at the surface above. She quickly used her arms to push herself back to the top.

She broke through the water and gave Kat a big grin. Kat started cheering and then Hanna realized that all the other campers, were all cheering and clapping for her! Hanna swam to the platform where several hands reached over to pull her up.

"Unbelievable!" exclaimed Kat. "I've never seen anyone go as high as you did!"

"Really?"

"Yeah," said another camper. "You were awesome."

Hanna heard someone calling her name and waved to Lily and Tiff who stood in the sand.

"You were great!" yelled Lily.

Then Tiff yelled, "Weren't you scared?"

"A little," Hanna yelled back, "but, it was worth it! You should try it!"

Hanna watched as Tiff took a few steps backwards and shook her head.

Hanna turned to Kat and said. "I'll be right back."

## TIFF

Tiff watched as Hanna ran across the hot sand to where she was standing.

"Hey," Hanna said as she pushed her wet hair out of her eyes. "You guys have to try this. It looks scary but it is *so* much fun!"

Tiff pushed her sunglasses up on her head and shrugged her shoulders as she said, "No, thanks. I might get hurt."

"Hurt? The worse that could happen is you get water up your nose!"

"My mom saw a picture of the Blob in the camp brochure and said if someone landed wrong in the water they could break an arm or something." Tiff looked directly at Hanna and continued, "I know you think pageants are stupid but they are important to me. I have a big pageant in August and I won't be able to compete if I have a cast on my arm."

"Look," replied Hanna. "I'm sorry about what I said about pageants. I've never been in one, so I guess I shouldn't have an opinion."

"Thanks," Tiff replied with a smile.

"Are you sure you don't want to try? Kat won't land hard if you don't want to go too high."

"You expect me to trust her?" Tiff exclaimed. "No way!"

"Fine, but you're missing out on a lot of fun," said Hanna as she turned and headed back to the lake.

Tiff could not believe that Hanna actually thought she was stupid enough to go on that blob thing with Kat. She was tempted to tell Lily about what Kat did last night but decided it was best not to be a tattletale since it would probably make things even worse. Besides, she could take care of herself so Kat had better watch out!

Tiff looked around and saw that Amy had still not made it down to the beach. Amy barely talked to anyone, but at least she wasn't mean and Tiff wanted someone to hang out with on the beach. Where was she?

"Lily, I'm going back to the trail to find Amy," she yelled.

Tiff shuffled through the sand until she reached the entrance to the rocky trail. She took a few steps into the shady trail and yelled, "Amy, where are you?"

I am not going too far back up this stupid trail, Tiff thought to herself. I'm trying to be nice by going out of my way to find Amy, but this Girl Scout hiking stuff is for the birds. As she walked gingerly up the rocky path listening for Amy's reply, a rustling noise in the bushes made her stop in her tracks.

"A snake," Tiff whispered, as she stayed frozen and stared at the bush.

A small pink nose and light brown fluff emerged and a small brown bunny poked out his head. The bunny saw Tiff and froze. They both stared at each other. Tiff slowly looked around for its mother. No other animal was in sight and she couldn't hear any rustling in the bushes. Tiff slowly dropped to her knees and carefully picked up the bunny. His fur was so soft and warm.

Tiff cuddled the tiny bunny as it trembled in her arms. "You poor little thing … all alone in the woods," Tiff whispered. "You are the cutest thing in the world!"

Tiff had never had a pet before. Her mom had said Tiff was too busy with important things to take care of a pet. At this moment, Tiff couldn't think of anything more important than taking care of this bunny. Where was Amy? Her mom was a veterinarian, so she would know how to take care of a bunny.

"Amy," Tiff yelled louder as the bunny trembled more. "I need your help! Where are you?"

## AMY

Amy didn't realize how terrified she was of the water until she had reached the edge of the trail and saw the lake ahead.

Blue glistening water stretched out as far as she could see. The lake reminded Amy of her fishing trips with her dad. They would camp out on the shore and then fish for dinner. She could still smell the fire they would make together with the branches she would gather up in the woods. Her dad would toss some baking potatoes wrapped in foil on the fire and then they would sit together to grill their fish.

Amy did not go on the last camping trip because she had strep throat. Instead, her dad went with a friend to fish on a lake and their boat flipped when it hit a stump under the water.

Amy turned away from the lake and headed back towards the cabin. She could not sit on the shore next to the lake. After a few steps, she heard someone calling her name. It sounded like Tiff. Amy thought for a moment and then decided she should at least find out what Tiff needed.

Amy turned back towards the lake and yelled, "Tiff, I am right here."

Tiff appeared on the trail in front of Amy with a furry bundle in her arms.

"There you are! Look what I found!" Tiff said anxiously as she hurried towards Amy. Amy reached out and took the small trembling bundle from Tiff. She started whispering to the tiny bunny while she held it close to her heart.

"What are you doing?" Tiff asked.

"I'm trying to calm it down," Amy explained. "It's really scared. I'm holding it close so it can feel my heart beating. Did you see the mother close by?"

"No," said Tiff, "I looked around but it looked like it was all alone."

"I think it's been alone for a few days," Amy said. "It seems weak, like it hasn't had any food or water."

"Did you learn this stuff from your mom or dad?" Tiff asked.

"Both," said Amy. "Since my mom is a vet she taught me more about domestic animals, like pets. But my dad taught me all about wild animals."

"Is your dad a park ranger or something?" asked Tiff.

"He used to be a photographer for a wildlife magazine," Amy explained. She tried to hold back the tears but she again thought of the lake below and tears starting streaming down her face. "But he died last year when he drowned in a boating accident on a lake."

Amy buried her face into the bunny and tried to cover her tears but it was too late.

She sobbed so hard that she was afraid she would scare the small bunny even more so she handed it back to Tiff.

"Wow," Tiff said quietly as she took the bunny. "I am so sorry about your dad."

## LILY

Lily was worried about Tiff and Amy so she left the beach and headed back up the trail towards the cabin when she spotted the two standing in the middle of the trail. She could tell even from a distance that something was wrong.

"Is everything okay?" Lily yelled as she started to run towards the girls.

Amy was hiding her face in her hands and sobbing. Lily was surprised to see Tiff holding a rabbit but she just gave her a curious look and then turned her attention to Amy.

"C'mon," she said calmly as she put her arm around Amy. "Let's go down to the lake and sit down so you can tell me what is wrong."

"I can't go near the water!" she sobbed.

"You don't have to go in the water," Lily said gently. "Just come sit with me. We will stay on the shore the whole time."

"She can't be near the lake," Tiff explained. "Her dad drowned and being close to the lake freaks her out."

"I am so sorry," Lily said to Amy. "Do you want me to take you back to the cabin?"

"Well," Tiff said as Amy continued to cry, "what ever you decide to do, you can't walk around with red puffy eyes."

Lily watched as Tiff handed Amy the bunny, took off her Chanel sunglasses and put them on Amy.

"There, that's better," Tiff announced as she stepped back to admire her work.

"Thanks, but I can't take your expensive glasses," Amy said softly as she started to hand the glasses back to Tiff.

"I'm not giving them to you," Tiff said. "I'm just letting you borrow them. Besides, they look better on you than on me."

Amy put the glasses on and smiled a little as she stopped crying and started to stroke the bunny. Lily took this opportunity to get Amy's mind off her dad and the lake. "Where did you guys find this adorable bunny?" she asked.

"I found it!" declared Tiff as she took the bunny back from Amy and held it tightly to her chest. "I'm going to keep it and call her Kee Kee. It's short for Cherokee."

"We aren't supposed to take wild animals from the woods," explained Lily. "I don't think you can keep it."

"That's not fair!" cried Tiff. "If I leave her out here she will die!"

Great, thought Lily. Now both of them are upset, how am I supposed to handle this situation? Should I make Tiff abandon a tiny bunny alone in the woods? Should I make Amy overcome her fear and take her down to the lake? Why is being a counselor so complicated?

Amy interrupted her thoughts when she suddenly said, "Lily, Tiff is right. I don't think it has a mother since it is so weak. It seems like it hasn't had any food or water for a couple of days."

"Okay," Lily said firmly as she made her decision. "We will take the bunny with us and I'll go talk to Mr. Donovan and see if you can keep him."

"Thanks, Lily," Tiff said gratefully, "Oh, and just so you know— it's not a *him,* it's a *her.*"

"How do you know it's a girl?" Lily asked as she began to wonder what her camp director would think about this latest development in Cabin #3.

"It doesn't matter," Tiff said. "It will still have a pink cage and a diamond collar, so I say it's a girl."

"This little bunny will certainly be spoiled," Lily said.

"Then it will take after its mother," a familiar voice said from behind.

They all turned around and found Kat and Hanna standing behind them dripping wet.

Tiff forgot all about being mad at Kat as she exclaimed, "Look what I found! Now we have two mascots for our cabin!"

Hanna ran right up to Tiff and started stroking the bunny. But Lily noticed that Kat was looking carefully at Amy, not the bunny. So she wasn't surprised when Kat asked, "What's wrong, Amy? You look like you've been crying a lot."

"Her dad drowned last year in a lake like this one," Tiff quickly explained.

"OMG!" said Hanna as her hand flew up to her mouth. "That's terrible."

"I'm really sorry," Kat said sincerely, "I can't imagine my dad.... dying."

They all stood in awkward silence. Lily needed to think of something fast.

"Let's grab our stuff and head back to the cabin," she said. "I will need to talk to Mr. Donovan about the bunny. We aren't supposed to take wild animals from the woods. But since it doesn't seem to have a mother to take care of it, I think we should be able to keep it in the cabin."

"Let's go back to the cabin right now and find her a cage or something," Tiff said.

"Wait!" Kat said, "Hanna really wanted you guys to see her fly off the Blob! She was awesome!"

"I don't think ..." Lily started.

"Being close to the lake freaks Amy out," Tiff interrupted.

"It's okay," Amy said softly. "I'll try to stand close enough to watch you, Hanna."

"Are you sure?" asked Lily.

"Yes," Amy said softly. "I really want to see this blob-thing."

Lily led the four back down the trail towards the lake. A lot of drama in this cabin, Lily thought to herself. But she had to admit, there was never a dull moment.

# THE CAMPFIRE

## HANNA

Hanna followed close behind the others down the trail towards the campfire. The smell of wood burning was sharp in the air and she could see peaks of smoke curling up over the trees into the gray sky. It was dusk and soon she would need to use her trusty Hello Kitty flashlight to see the trail.

It was the end of her first week of camp and so far, so good. She had conquered the Blob, learned how to shoot a bow and arrow, and tried to row a canoe. She was also learning how to ride a horse. The first time they went to the horse stables, she was so scared. The horses were huge and she was scared to death to climb up on one. However, the instructor was patient and spent a lot of time explaining how to sit properly in the saddle and how to use the reins and the pressure of her feet to steer the horse.

But today was Hanna's favorite day so far. It was Indian Lore day and they had learned all about the Cherokee Indians—the tribe the camp was named after! Hanna even made a "Dream Catcher" out of feathers. She was supposed to hang it above her bed at home, and it would catch all of her good dreams and keep away any nightmares. How cool was that?

Tonight the entire camp was gathering at the campfire to roast marshmallows. Since the campfire was cancelled on the first night of camp, this was the first time Hanna would roast a marshmallow. She didn't quite understand what all the excitement was about. She would rather curl in beanbag chair in the Cyber Corner and look up more info about the Cherokee Indians than sit in front of a smoky fire.

"Tell me again why we are doing this?" Hanna called up to the others.

"Because it is fun," said Kat. "You *really* need to get a life!"

"Did you just tell me to GAL?" Hanna demanded.

"If GAL stands for get a life then, yes!" Kat replied.

"I have a life, thank you very much. Trudging through the woods to sit outside by a hot fire does not sound like fun to me," Hanna said.

"Doesn't sound like fun to me either," agreed Tiff. "But I really want to try those S'more things."

"Some more things?" Hanna asked, wondering if she heard Tiff correctly.

"S'more!" yelled Kat. "Everyone knows what those are! They are as American as apple pie!"

"Well, I don't like apple pie either," said Hanna, "so I doubt I will like these some more things."

"Of course you'll like them," Amy said. "Everyone loves them—that's why they're called S'mores because you will ask to have some more."

"I think I will pass since I have no idea what the ingredients are," Hanna replied.

"Hanna, for someone who is so smart," said Kat, "you can be pretty dumb sometimes. You make a S'more by taking a marshmallow and roasting it over the fire. Then you take two graham crackers and put a piece of a Hershey chocolate bar and the toasted marshmallow in between the two crackers. Then, you smash it together and eat it! It taste great and there's nothing in it that will make you sick!"

"I am not dumb," Hanna said with a huff. "I just think the whole campfire experience is stupid."

"That's your problem," said Kat. "You think too much. Stop thinking and start doing!"

Hanna started to remind Kat that she had gone on the Blob. Didn't that count for something?

But Hanna knew deep inside, that Kat was right. She was way too serious. She didn't want to take any risks so she missed out on a lot of fun. She decided she would try one of these strange crackers and she would try to enjoy the campfire without analyzing the situation, like the intensity of the heat or the direction of the flames as the wind whipped through the pine trees. She would try to take Kat's advice— she would stop thinking so much and start doing more.

## TIFF

"Making S'mores sounds messy," Tiff suddenly said. "I guess I shouldn't have worn my white shirt tonight."

"You dress way too fancy for a camp," Kat said to Tiff.

"Well you just need to mind your own business sometimes," said Tiff. "Not everyone wants to hear your opinion."

Tiff walked faster to get away from Kat. As she rounded a curve in the trail, the campfire appeared before her with orange and red flames dancing in the air. Surrounding the round fire pit were large rocks. Outside of the pit were rows of benches made of tree trunks sliced in half.

Groups of campers were piling into the area and claiming their seats close to the fire. Tiff could see Lily on the other side of the fire saving a front row, waving her arms. Tiff hurried towards Lily with the others trailing close behind.

"Hey guys!" Lily said as they reached the bench. She held up a huge basket and said, "Here's all the stuff we need to make S'mores. Dig in!"

Kat and Amy were like pros, thought Tiff, as she watched them grab their supplies and sit down on the bench near the fire. Tiff looked over at Hanna who shrugged and reached her hand into the basket. Tiff reached in too and grabbed a few graham crackers and a Hershey bar. She then grabbed a whole bag of marshmallows and looked up at Lily for some instructions but Lily had already walked away to the other side of the fire to talk to some other counselors.

Tiff went and stood next to Amy who was sitting down and putting a marshmallow on the end of a stick. Tiff looked down at the wooden bench that looked like a rotten tree stump.

"Aren't there any chairs?" Tiff asked. There must be a lawn chair or something around here, she thought to herself. She put the bag of marshmallows on the ground behind her and looked around.

"You have got to be kidding," said Kat who was sitting next to Amy. "This is a campfire, not a dining room!"

"Excuse me for having higher standards than you!" Tiff yelled at Kat.

"Yeah, you have high standards—higher than your IQ," Hanna mumbled.

"What did you say?" asked Tiff with a hurt expression on her face.

"Sorry," said Hanna. "You are just so … unbelievable, at times."

"Just because Kat knows more about the outdoors than me does not mean that she is smarter than me, or has a higher IQ than me," declared Tiff. "I know a lot of things, too!"

## KAT

"Do you know much about raccoons?" asked Kat.

"Raccoons? What does that have to do with anything?" Tiff said in a frustrated voice.

"Well," said Kat, "it has to do a lot with your marshmallows since one just snuck away with your whole bag."

"What?" squealed Tiff as she jumped up on the bench and looked around.

Kat pointed to a small bush that was moving slightly and then burst out laughing with Amy. The bag of marshmallows was gone and there were tiny paw prints in the dirt leading to the bushes. Kat watched as Amy walked over the bush, kneeled and looked at the prints.

"Yep," she confirmed. "It was a raccoon."

"I told you!" said Kat. "I saw it run away while Tiff was blabbing on about how smart she was."

"Why didn't you stop that thief!" cried Tiff. "He has my marsh-mallows!"

"Here," said Hanna as she held out another bag. "We have plenty left."

Tiff stayed up on the bench and said, "Aren't you guys scared? It might come back and bite us and give us rabies."

What a sissy, thought Kat.

"The way you're carrying on, it probably thinks you have rabies!" said Kat as she held up her stick with a brown marshmallow on the end.

"Look," Kat said proudly, "this marshmallow is perfect!"

"It's not perfect, it's burnt," said Tiff as she climbed carefully down from the bench and sat down. "You think you are so smart and you can't even cook a marshmallow."

"Fine, Miss Smarty Pants," Kat said. "You try it."

"Fine, I will," said Tiff as she sat down next to Hanna.

"It can't be rocket science," Kat heard Hanna say to Tiff.

Kat watched as both Hanna and Tiff put a marshmallow on the end of their sticks and placed them into the flames. Within seconds, both marshmallows burst out in flames. Kat squealed with laughter as both girls dropped their sticks and jumped back from the fire. Amy jumped up and rescued both sticks from the flames.

"Maybe we should help them a little," Amy whispered to Kat.

"Fine," replied Kat, "you take the Marshmallow Brain and I'll take … the Brain."

## AMY

Amy sat with Tiff and showed her how to hold the stick just over the hot coals, not directly in the flames. She also showed her how to turn the stick around so that each side was evenly toasted.

Tiff caught on quickly but decided she liked them without the chocolate. Less mess to worry about, she had told Amy. Plus, they were delicious without the chocolate!

Amy loved to sit around the campfire at night. She could hear the symphony of crickets in the darkness and an owl hooting in the distance. Through the trees, she could see fireflies dancing in and out of the shadows. She looked above her to the sky. It looked like a black blanket with sparkling white gems. As she started to think about all of her camping trips with her dad, someone across the fire started singing.

Amy knew the song so she joined in with the others. Kat, of course, knew all the words too, and was singing as loud as she could. Tiff and Hanna just sat and listened. Amy decided that tomorrow she would write down the words of the song for them so they could sing along, too, at the next campfire.

She wanted so much for the girls in her cabin to get along with each other. Sure, the other girls got on her nerves but she just ignored them. Of course, they ignored her too, but Amy was used to being left out so it didn't bother her too much.

Once the sing along was over, and everyone was stuffed with S'mores, they helped clean up the leftovers and headed back to the cabin. They were all exhausted from the busy day and walked slowly back to their cabin.

As they got ready for bed, Amy was glad that her cabin mates were too tired tonight to argue with each other. Soon they would need to work together on a play for the last night of camp—which was the end of next week! How could they practice a play if they couldn't even get along for more than five minutes?

# THE GHOST

## HANNA

Hanna woke up to a light shining in her eyes and Tiff screaming, "There's a ghost! Wake up!"

"What?" Hanna whispered, trying to untangle herself from her blanket.

"Look," said Tiff, pointing out the window. "It's moving away from our cabin but it was right outside our window!"

Hanna climbed out of the top bunk and stood next to Tiff to look through the window. A tap on her shoulder caused Hanna to jump. She bumped into Tiff and they both screamed but stopped when they heard Amy's voice in the dark, "What is going on? And where is Kat?"

"Kat?" Hanna questioned. "You mean she's not in her bunk?"

"No," said Amy. "I never heard her get up. I just heard Tiff scream."

"Gimme your flashlight," Hanna demanded as she grabbed it from Tiff's hand and went over to Kat's bed. She shone the light on the bottom bunk but all she saw was a comforter crumpled up in a pile next to her pillow. This isn't good, she thought to herself. She put her hand on the middle of the bed. It was still warm.

"She hasn't been gone very long," she declared.

"What are you? A detective or something?" said Tiff as she took her flashlight back. "The ghost probably snatched her and is dragging her through the woods to the...."

"Maybe Kat is the ghost," Amy said.

"Kat is a ghost?" gasped Tiff. "I knew there was something weird about her ..."

"There is no such thing as a ghost," Hanna said firmly.

"Oh yeah?" replied Tiff nervously, "I saw a TV show once about a haunted house and they filmed some ghosts floating around."

"I thought you couldn't take a picture of a ghost," said Amy.

"There is no such thing as a ghost!" Hanna said louder. "You didn't see a ghost on TV either. They use lights, mirrors, and technical stuff to make it look like a ghost."

"Don't yell at me," said Tiff. "Amy is the one who said Kat was a ghost."

## AMY

Amy took a breath and said, "What I meant to say is that maybe the thing you saw in the woods is not a ghost, but Kat."

"But why would Kat be in the woods in the middle of the night?" whined Tiff. "I still think something snatched her and ..."

"She probably had to GGP and she's in the outhouse," said Hanna.

"Oh, don't remind me," Tiff said, crossing her legs. "That's what woke me up—I have to go really bad."

"You will have to hold it until we find Kat," Hanna replied as she reached for her Hello Kitty slippers. "C'mon, let's go."

"Are you crazy?" Tiff said. "There is no way I would go out there!"

"Then stay here," said Amy, knowing that Tiff would never stay in the cabin by herself at night.

"Alone, with a ghost close by?" exclaimed Tiff as she grabbed her pink fluffy bedroom slippers. "I'm coming, too."

Amy looked around for her shoes and glanced over at Rascal's cage. He was happily chewing on a carrot in the corner of his cage. She glanced at Kee Kee, curled up asleep in the corner of her cage. Maybe Kat felt like she was in a cage and needed to get out of the cabin.

Amy found her tennis shoes and quickly slipped them on as she grabbed her flashlight. "I'm ready," she said. "Let's go find Kat!"

## LILY

As they headed out into the dark, they saw a light quickly coming up the path and Lily appeared before them with a flashlight.

"What is all the commotion?" Lily asked in a worried tone. "I could hear you all the way from my cabin!"

"We were just coming to get you," Hanna explained. "Kat is missing ..."

"And there is a ghost in the woods!" interrupted Tiff. "It was right outside my window but I think I scared it away with my flashlight. It floated that way," she said, pointing in the direction of the woods.

Lily's heart started to pound. Kat was missing? She had to be close by. They would look for her in the woods around the cabin but if they didn't find her within a few minutes Lily would need to notify Mr. Donovan.

"We need to find her," she said. "Amy, can you run back to the cabin and get me a blanket?"

"Sure," said Amy as she headed back into the cabin.

"I'll come with you!" said Hanna yelled after Amy as she followed her down the path.

As they stood alone in the dark Lily said to Tiff, "I'm glad you came out here to help."

Lily watched as Tiff squirmed and said, "Well, she's a pain but she is my cabin mate. I just hope this experience doesn't haunt me the rest of my life!"

Lily smiled weakly and replied, "I doubt it will haunt you but it will certainly be something you will remember for a long, long time!"

## KAT

Kat must be dreaming. She heard voices calling her name and she felt like she was floating. She could feel herself shivering and her bare feet crunching on something hard and cold. Suddenly, she realized she was standing in the middle of the woods!

"Oh, no," groaned Kat as she wrapped her arms around her chest to keep warm. "I was sleepwalking!"

Her mother would be so upset if she found out. Kat had started sleepwalking several months ago but then she went a whole month without sleepwalking. Her mom thought she had outgrown this stage and allowed Kat to go to camp away from her watchful eye.

"I probably had too much caffeine after eating all those S'mores," Kat mumbled to herself.

Kat wondered how far from the cabin she had wandered. She tried to look through the dark for signs of the path. The stars were bright and the moon cast an eerie glow through the thick trees. As she struggled with deciding which way to go, she heard faint voices again in the distance.

"Here I am," she yelled.

The voices got louder and Lily appeared before her with Kat's three cabin mates close behind.

"Are you okay?" Lily asked as she wrapped a blanket around Kat's shoulders.

"You scared us to death!" Tiff said. "I saw you through the window and thought you were a ghost. Of course, I know ghosts aren't real but ..."

"Why are you out here alone in the dark?" demanded Hanna. "This isn't a smart thing to do."

"I didn't mean to be outside," explained Kat. "I was sleepwalking." Kat turned to Lily and pleaded, "Please don't tell my mom or she will make me go home."

"Sleepwalking!" Tiff said in awe. "That is so cool. I never met someone who could walk in her sleep. How do you see where you are going with your eyes closed?"

"Her eyes are not closed when she is sleepwalking," explained Hanna, "It's kind of like her body is awake but her mind is asleep."

"Let's talk about it some more over a cup of hot chocolate," said Lily as she put her arm around Kat and steered her in the direction of the cabin. "We need to get you warmed up."

"Um ... no more chocolate, please," Kat said. "I think it was all the chocolate bars I ate with my S'Mores—too much caffeine sometimes makes me sleepwalk."

"I have great idea!" Amy said excitedly. "We can make reindeer milk!"

"Gross!" wailed Tiff. "I refuse to drink milk from a reindeer! First, a huge spider attacks me, then I have to take a shower with a slimy lizard, then a raccoon steals my stuff and now you want me to drink from a reindeer! I can't handle all this wildlife!"

"Well if you can't handle wildlife, I guess you better not keep Kee Kee," Kat said in a serious tone.

"Kee Kee is not wild!" exclaimed Tiff. "She is perfectly tame."

"Stop arguing," said Lily. "Tiff, you don't have to get rid of Kee Kee and Amy is not talking about milk from an actual reindeer."

"Yeah," explained Amy. "It's just regular milk warmed up with sugar and dash of vanilla. My dad used to make it for me all the time when we were camping."

"It sounds great!" said Kat. "As long as there is no chocolate—I definitely do not want to get up again tonight!"

"But Rascal would be happy to find out that you're nocturnal, too!" kidded Amy. "You can both stay up all night!"

"No, thanks," said Kat with a laugh. "I love Rascal but he's on his own tonight. Once I hit the pillow I will be out for the rest of tonight."

## TIFF

Good, Tiff thought to herself. The sooner Kat goes to sleep, the sooner I can pay her back for scaring me the first night of camp. Tiff had been waiting for the perfect opportunity and tonight was the night.

When they reached the cabin, Lily told them to go in and settle down while she went to the Dining Hall to get some hot drinks. Once they warmed up, they settled back down in their bunk beds and Lily went back to her own cabin.

All the lights were off as Tiff told her a ghost story in the scariest voice she could muster. She had been telling ghost stories every night and was running out of new stories to tell. She stopped the story to rearrange her comforter when she realized the cabin was very quiet— too quiet. The only noise was the heavy breathing of her cabin mates and the chirping of crickets outside.

"Hey," she whispered sharply. "Are you guys still awake?" No response came from the bed above her or from the other bunk.

A sharp scratching noise came from across the room. Tiff froze and strained her ears to listen. She then breathed a sigh of relief as she reminded herself that it was Rascal or Kee Kee.

Tiff shivered at the thought of putting her feet down on the cold wooden floor but she was determined to go through with her plan. She took the bottle of red nail polish from under her pillow and climbed out of bed. She then tiptoed quietly over to Kat's bed and leaned in closely to listen. Kat was lying on her back and was breathing heavily. She was sound asleep with one foot sticking out from under her comforter.

Perfect, Tiff said to herself as she got to work. It was hard to see in the dark but the moon was bright and cast just enough light for Tiff to paint each toenail bright fire engine red. Tiff carefully lifted up the comforter and painted the toenails on the other foot. She then carefully painted each of Kat's fingernails. She tried not to giggle when she thought of Kat's reaction when she woke up and saw her surprise.

"I told you I would get you back," Tiff mumbled to herself as she tiptoed back into her bed and fell into a deep sleep.

# THE CAKE

## KAT

Kat woke up and heard the rain outside. She remembered her sleep-walking incident last night and was glad she was safe and dry in the cabin. She was a little worried about what her mom would say if Lily called and told her what happened.

Kat reached down to straighten her comforter when she gasped. Her fingernails were painted red! She instantly knew that Tiff was behind this.

"You are dead meat!" she screamed as she jumped out of bed.

"What?" she heard Hanna mumble. "Who's dead?"

"Tiff is," Kat yelled, "as soon as I get my hands on her!"

Kat ran over to Tiff's bed and pulled off her comforter.

"Hey," Tiff said as she tried to pull her comforter back over her. "Stop it. I am trying to sleep."

"What is going on?" asked Amy who was up now and standing next to Hanna yawning.

"Ask the princess here," said Kat as she stood over Tiff with her arms across her chest.

"What's the matter?" mumbled Tiff. "Don't you like the color I picked out for you?"

"What is she talking about?" Hanna asked looking confused.

"This!" exclaimed Kat as she held out her hands. "She painted my fingernails while I was sleeping!"

"Well," said Amy, "it is a pretty color."

Tiff sat up and smiled, "I thought so. And it matches her toes."

"My toes!" screamed Kat as she looked down at her feet.

"Don't worry," said Hanna, "it will come off."

Kat ran to the sink and started washing her hands, scrubbing her nails with a paper towel.

"It doesn't come off with just soap and water," Tiff yelled across the cabin. "You need polish remover which I believe is *not* available here at this wonderful camp. I believe I have the only bottle of remover."

Kat turned from the sink and walked back to Tiff. "Okay, you got me back. Now can I please use some of your polisher remover stuff?"

"Nope," Tiff said as she climbed out of her bed. "I think it looks good on you. Just be glad I didn't have any scissors or I would've given you a haircut instead."

"You wouldn't dare!"

"Try me," said Tiff as she glared at Kat.

"Okay, you two," said Amy. "You both played a trick on each other so now you are even. Can you stop fighting now?"

Tiff and Kat stood and glared at each other.

"Fine," said Tiff, "we will call it even."

"Not until you take this polish off my nails," said Kat.

"Nope," said Tiff. "Think of the positive side of this—it might help you stop biting your nails."

"I like biting my nails," Kat grumbled. Kat knew that she would have to be nice to Tiff if she wanted this paint off her nails so she said, "You win. I will wear the polish today but if you take it off my nails tonight then I will call it even."

"Promise?" asked Tiff.

"Promise," said Kat.

"Pinky promise?" asked Tiff.

"Don't push it," said Kat as she turned away and went to her trunk to change for breakfast.

As Kat pulled out a t-shirt, Tiff yelled from her bunk, "Make sure you pick out a red shirt to match your nails!"

Kat held up a fist and said, "How about I make your nose red to match my nails?"

"Kat, stop acting so tough," said Amy. "You know you would never actually hit her."

"Guys," said Hanna, "I am starving. Can we please go eat breakfast?"

## HANNA

Hanna was really getting tired of Kat and Tiff constantly fighting. Couldn't they at least pretend to get along? Hanna led the way as the four walked down the path towards the Dining Hall for breakfast.

It was still early in the morning and the sun was hiding behind dark clouds. They each had a flashlight and the beams of light danced in front of them. The flickering lights reminded Hanna of candles on a birthday cake.

"I just had a great idea!" she said as stopped on the trail and turned around. "I heard another camp counselor say that tomorrow is Lily's birthday. Her parents are coming tonight to take her out to dinner so we should make her a cake while she is gone!"

"A cake?" Amy asked, "I've never made a cake before. Do you know how?"

"It would be NP. We just get the stuff from the kitchen, mix it up and bake it." Hanna said.

"Great idea!" said Kat. "Remember when we were talking about what our favorite food was? Lily said that Angel Food Cake was her favorite so that's what we should make."

"But we don't have a recipe," Amy reminded her.

"Let me set up my laptop in the Cyber Corner and I'll STW for the recipe." Hanna said.

They reached the Dining Hall and Hanna ran straight to the Cyber Corner. A few minutes later she joined the others at a table and announced, "Here are the ingredients.... egg whites, sugar, flour and a little salt. That's it! You don't have to be a G9 to make this cake!"

"I don't know," whined Tiff. "It sounds like a lot of work to me."

"Just breathing in and out is a lot of work for you," Kat said.

"Can't we just make her a card or something?" asked Amy.

"Making a cake will be fun!" said Kat. "We can sneak back here tonight after dinner and use the kitchen!"

"SLAP!" said Hanna.

"SLAP? That's means *sounds like a plan*, right?" asked Kat.

"Right," said Hanna.

"We might get in trouble," Amy said with a worried expression on her face.

"It would be worth it," said Kat. "Just think about how happy Lily will be when we give her the cake!"

## TIFF

Later that evening, Tiff sat at the edge of her bunk listening to the raindrops fall on the roof of the cabin. There had been no outside activities today because of the steady downpour of rain. They had spent the day inside doing crafts—tie-dye, basket weaving, pottery and making bead necklaces.

"So," said Tiff, happy to be safe inside the cabin, "do you want to play Charades or should I tell some ghost stories?"

"Anything but your stupid ghost stories!" moaned Kat as she tried to pick off more polish from her nails.

"I could paint little flowers on your toenails!" offered Tiff.

"No way," Kat said. "And don't forget you promised to take this polish off my nails before we go to bed tonight."

"We are supposed to take this time to write letters to our parents," said Hanna.

"My parents aren't even home so I won't waste my time," said Tiff.

"We still have some time before we can sneak back into the Dining Hall, so let's think of something to do," Tiff said.

"Why don't we talk about our play?" suggested Amy. "We need to decide what we are going to do."

"I don't want to be in any play," announced Hanna.

"I don't want to be in it either," said Amy. "I am terrified about getting up in front of all those people."

"Oh, c'mon guys!" cried Tiff. "It will be so much fun!"

"She's right," said Kat. "I hate to agree with princess here, but the camp plays are a lot of fun. Everyone makes a fool of themselves."

"I prefer not to make a fool of myself," replied Hanna, "so I will stay behind the scenes."

"And, I don't have any talent," said Amy. "I can't sing or dance or anything."

"Kat and I can't do the play by ourselves!" exclaimed Tiff.

"Well, you did tell us you were very talented so I am sure you can handle it by yourself," said Hanna. "After all, you are Miss Popular!"

"Popular—that's a great idea!" exclaimed Tiff. "We can sing the song, "Popular" from *Wicked*!"

Tiff saw the puzzled faces and said, "You know, from the Broadway play?"

"I have no idea what you are talking about, but I am not singing any stupid song about some girl who is popular," Kat said with disgust.

"I heard of that play," said Hanna. "It came to Atlanta last year."

"It is the story of the Wicked Witch and the Good Witch in the *Wizard of Oz*," explained Tiff. "The story takes place when the witches were teenage girls in boarding school!"

Tiff was so excited and she could see the scene in her mind. It was perfect! "The play has this amazing song called "Popular" which would be great for our play! I won't tell you the whole story because you really need to see it."

"Let me guess," asked Kat. "You will be the one singing the song?"

"Well, yeah," said Tiff. "I would sing it directly to one of you so it will be kind of like a play. The song is from one scene where the good witch is trying to make the wicked witch change the way she dresses and the way she acts so she will be more popular."

"It still sounds stupid to me," said Kat. "The play is supposed to be funny. Its not supposed to be the story of *your* life."

"My life? Are you calling *me* a witch?" demanded Tiff.

"You said it, not me ...," replied Kat.

## HANNA

"Don't start arguing!" Hanna said. "Let's go back the Dining Hall and see if everyone is gone so we can make the cake."

It was still raining hard so they grabbed their plastic ponchos and flashlights and headed out the door. They could tell from a distance that the Dining Hall was dark and quiet. The assistant counselors had finished cleaning and the side door was unlocked for late night snacks and supervised visits to the fridge.

"You know that a counselor is supposed to be with us when we come here at night," explained Amy.

"We know," said Hanna, "but if Lily comes with us, the cake won't be a surprise!"

"Yeah," added Kat, "so let's try to leave the lights out and just use our flashlights so no one sees us."

The side door opened easily and the four entered the large dark room.

"It's kind of spooky in there," Tiff said as she took a step inside and stopped.

"Well, you can stay here and guard the door if you like," Hanna said.

"Sure," said Tiff as she took her post by the door while the other girls headed into the dark kitchen.

"I'll get the stuff from the fridge," said Hanna as she used her flashlight to guide her.

"Okay," said Kat as she read the recipe with her flashlight, "the first step is to separate the eggs."

Hanna put the eggs on the counter and then watched as Kat moved the eggs around on the counter with a puzzled expression on her face.

"Separate the eggs?" asked Kat. "They are separate. They aren't hooked together or anything."

Amy and Hanna both continued to watch Kat as she picked up each egg and look at it carefully.

"Why are you staring at me?" Kat asked.

"We're just admiring your red fingernails," Hanna said with a giggle.

"Yeah, right," said Kat as she continued to move the eggs around.

Hanna and Amy both burst out laughing.

"I don't get it!" Kat said in an exasperated tone. "These eggs are already separated!"

"It means," Hanna started to explain while she tried to stop laughing, "to separate the egg yolks from the egg whites. I help my mom do this when we make omelets."

"Fine," Kat said in a huff. "You and Amy make the stupid cake since you are both a couple of smarty-pants. I'll help the princess guard the door."

## AMY

"Don't be mad," Amy said. "We didn't mean to laugh at you."

"Humph," Kat replied and marched over to her post next to Tiff.

"Let her go," Hanna said loudly. "We can make the cake and then Kat and Tiff can clean up."

"I heard that!" Kat yelled over her shoulder. "I am not cleaning up! Been there—done that! Not gonna happen!"

"I just love this teamwork," Amy yelled back in a sarcastic tone as she started cracking open the eggs. "I always get stuck with the work."

"Really?" said Hanna as she edged in next to Amy and started to measure the sugar. "Same with me—the quiet smart girls do all the work while the loud sporty girls and the pretty popular girls get off easy."

"My mom calls them 'blister sisters" since they show up after the work is done," Amy said.

"Blister sisters!" laughed Hanna. "That's a good one!"

Hanna helped Amy mix up the batter and pour it into the pan. While the cake baked in the oven, they washed and cut up strawberries and found a tub of whipped cream in the freezer.

As they worked, Amy thought about how she let people take advantage of her. She had always been a little shy, but ever since her dad died, she had become afraid to talk to people and it seemed like everyone pushed her around.

No more, she said to herself. I need to start standing up for myself.

Amy took a deep breath and walked over to Tiff and Kat. Hanna followed close behind.

"Hey guys, I've decided that I am not going to be a pushover anymore," she announced.

"That's great!" said Tiff. "We are behind you 100%."

"Good," replied Amy, "because I'm starting with you."

"What?" Tiff exclaimed with a horrified look on her face.

"And you," Amy continued as she nodded at Kat. "Hanna and I made the cake but, we are *not* washing the dishes."

She stared into the two shocked faces and added, "We bake and you guys clean. Fair?"

Tiff glanced over at Kat and shrugged. "Okay," Tiff said reluctantly.

"Yeah," Kat shrugged, "I guess that's fair."

As Amy walked back to the kitchen, Hanna smiled and gave her a thumbs up. Amy felt good. She was determined that she was not going to let people push her around anymore. She was not going to be afraid anymore.

Maybe tomorrow, she would even take a swim in the lake!

# THE CHANGES

## TIFF

A buzzer went off and Hanna said, "The cake is done!"

Tiff followed as everyone ran to the oven and watched Hanna take the cake out and place it on the counter.

"Wow!" Tiff exclaimed, "it looks great!"

"We need to let it cool before we take it out of the pan," Hanna said. "Let's go wait in the Cyber Corner."

As everyone piled onto the beanbag chairs, Tiff started to think about her life and all the things she took for granted. She had parents who cared about her, a beautiful house, lots of clothes and exciting vacations. She wondered how her life would be if she were living with a single mom, like Amy or having to share her things with three brothers, like Kat. She definitely could not imagine being cooped up in the house doing homework all the time, like Hanna.

I do have a great life, Tiff said to herself.

"Hey guys," she said, "since Amy is going to change, so am I."

"Change what?" asked Kat. "Your hairstyle?"

"No!" Tiff raised her voice above the giggles. "I am going to try to not whine and complain so much."

The giggling stopped and the girls stared at Tiff as she continued, "I am going to appreciate what I have and not act so...."

As Tiff struggled to find the word she was looking for, Kat chimed in and asked, "Spoiled?"

Tiff looked a bit hurt but then she surprised them all as she smiled and said, "Yes … spoiled. I am going to try and not act so spoiled."

"Good," said Hanna, "because you do act spoiled. But of course, everything does come easy to you."

"That's not true!" said Tiff. "My life is not easy! I have to take ballet and singing lessons twice a week and every Saturday I am in some sort of dance performance or beauty pageant. I have to always look perfect and I never have time to play and…."

"Wow, rough life," Kat interrupted in a sarcastic tone. "It must be hard to be so perfect all of the time."

Tiff saw that she still had everyone's attention so she ignored Kat's comment and kept talking. "Then, on Sunday we go to church and to my grandma's house for a formal dinner. Where, of course, I have to wear a dress and I am expected to sit up straight and use my best manners."

"Well," joked Kat, "why don't you just flick a forkful of food across the table? Then you would never be invited back and you could stay home and eat pizza!"

"I wish," replied Tiff, "but if I did that, then my mother would just put me back in charm school to work on my manners!"

"Charm school?" Hanna asked. "Those schools actually exist?"

"Yes," said Tiff. "I am a graduate of The Elite School for Young Ladies. Of course, you would never guess by looking at me now." She pushed her hair out of her face added, "I mean, look at me—I'm a mess!"

## KAT

"Being messy is fun!" declared Kat. "All the fun games are messy. Like baseball, when you get to slide into home plate in the dirt. Or football, when you get tackled in the mud."

"I can't imagine that getting dirty can be fun," Tiff smirked. "My parents would never allow me to play a game where I got dirty. My mom would have a fit."

"So," asked Kat, "I guess this means you've never played a game of paint ball?"

"No ..." replied Tiff slowly, "is this some kind of game you made up?"

"No, I didn't make it up," said Kat. "My brothers and I play in the woods behind my house. But there are places you can go to rent the paint guns and a place to play."

"Play ..." Tiff asked in an astonished tone, "with guns?"

"Not real guns," explained Kat, "but guns that shoot blobs of paint."

Amy stepped forward and asked, "So, everyone runs around in the woods and shoots paint at each other?"

"Yes!" Kat grinned. "It is so much fun. You guys need to come to my house and we can play."

## HANNA

"I still don't get the point," Hanna said. "You run around and shoot paint. Why?"

"Why?" Kat repeated, "Because it's fun!"

"Doesn't sound like fun to me," said Hanna.

"Or me," added Tiff.

Kat looked at both Tiff and Hanna and asked, "What do you guys think is fun?"

Tiff immediately replied and said, "It is really fun to compete in pageants."

The room was quiet as everyone stared at Hanna. Hanna thought about her days filled with studying and working on school projects.

"I guess I don't have much 'fun' if you are referring to mindless, silly activities. Fun to me is using my brain to figure something out," Hanna said.

"So," said Amy, "you probably like to do puzzles for fun."

"Yes," replied Hanna with a sense of relief. "I like puzzles and brain teasers. That's what I do for fun."

"I still think you would like to play paint ball," said Kat.

"Fine," said Hanna, "I'll make a deal with you, Kat. I will play paint ball if you go to charm school."

Tiff and Amy cracked up laughing at the thought of Kat wearing a dress and learning to cross her ankles and sip tea from a cup.

"That's not fair," replied Kat. "A game of paint ball lasts one hour and charm school is like every...."

Tiff interrupted and explained, "its two hours every week for eight weeks."

"Okay, here's the deal," Kat said to Hanna. "I will go to charm school if you join a local sports team that practices about two hours every week. You can choose basketball, softball, tennis or soccer."

Hanna panicked. Why did she challenge Kat like that? Now the girls expected her to come through with the deal. She took a deep breath and stuck her hand out to Kat.

"Deal," Hanna said hesitantly.

Hanna and Kat shook hands as Tiff and Amy grinned and clapped.

"I think you should try tennis," said Tiff. "You get to wear these cute little white skirts...."

"She's not going to pick a sport based on how cute the clothes are!" Kat exclaimed.

"Well you are going to need new clothes too, Kat," said Tiff. "You have to wear fancy dresses and white gloves when you go to etiquette class."

"Etta—what?" asked Kat. "I said I would go to charm school, not some class I can't even pronounce. And the only glove I will ever wear is a baseball glove!"

"Etiquette!" exclaimed Hanna. "It means manners. And if I have to wear ugly sports clothes then you have to wear a dress and white fancy gloves."

"Fine," Kat said to Hanna with a huff. "I'll wear the stupid dress and go to this stupid charm class. But, you should be scared, very scared."

Hanna looked nervously at Kat. "Why should I be scared?"

"Cause girls like you get eaten alive out on the field," Kat said as she put her hands behind her head and leaned back into the beanbag. "I bet you won't last a week."

"I will so!" exclaimed Hanna, but deep inside she wasn't so sure. Charm school couldn't be too difficult. How hard could it be to hold a teacup and stick out your pinky? But, sports camp? This was going to be hard!

I'm in trouble, Hanna said to herself, big trouble.

## AMY

"My mom almost enrolled me in a charm school last year," Amy suddenly said. "She thought it would help me in 'social situations' so I wouldn't be so shy."

"So," Tiff asked, "Why didn't you go?"

"Because ..." Amy said slowly as she started to laugh, "I was too shy!"

Amy's laugh was contagious. Tiff and Kat laughed along with her but Amy noticed that Hanna was quiet and looked a little worried.

"Don't worry," Amy leaned over and said to Hanna. "You will do fine in a sports camp."

"Thanks," said Hanna, not sounding too sure of herself.

Amy tried to think of something to get Hanna's mind off the sports camp. She then remembered their play and said, "Hey, Tiff can you sing us the song you said we should do in the play?"

"Sure," said Tiff. She stood up straight and sang in a clear, high voice:

*Popular*
*You're gonna be popular*
*I'll teach you the proper poise*
*To talk to boys*
*Everything you need to know to be*
*Popular*

"Wow," said Amy. "You really have a great voice!"

"Thanks," Tiff replied. "There's a lot more to the song, but do you like it so far?"

"Yes," said Amy. "I think it would be great for the skit!"

"I like it, too," Hanna said, "but I can't sing."

"Then you can be the technical director!" Tiff exclaimed.

"Okay," agreed Hanna. "I can download the song onto my laptop and hook it up to the speakers."

"Maybe I can be the other witch that you sing to," suggested Amy. "I am definitely not popular and I sure don't know how to talk to boys."

"You would be perfect!" Tiff agreed.

"What about me?" complained Kat. "I can't sing or dance but I'm not technical, either."

"What about a narrator?" suggested Amy.

"Great idea!" said Tiff. "Since most of the campers have not seen the play, Kat can stand up front and explain the scene."

"She won't even need a microphone!" said Hanna.

"Are you saying that I am loud?" Kat asked.

"Well," Tiff began, "you do a great job projecting your voice."

"Yep, she means you are a loudmouth," added Hanna.

"But that's a good thing!" Tiff tried to explain. "A lot of people, like Amy, don't project their voice so no one can hear them."

"Gee, thanks," said Amy softly.

"I'm sorry," said Tiff. "I didn't mean to hurt your feelings."

"That's okay," said Amy. "You're right. I do need to project my voice more so people will notice me. Maybe you can teach me some things your voice teacher showed you?"

"Sure!" Tiff said. "Since we have to wait for the cake to cool maybe we can start practicing."

"I can start downloading the song," offered Hanna.

"See if you can find me the story online so I can figure out what I need to say as the narrator," said Kat as she looked over Hanna's shoulder at the laptop.

Finally, thought Amy, no one is fighting! We are actually working together—like friends! She joined the others as they huddled around the laptop looking for information on *Wicked*. Amy crossed her fingers behind her back as she made a wish.... that they would all still friends in the morning!

# THE SURPRISE

## AMY

Amy woke up with the sun shining in her eyes. She stretched and looked around at her friends sprawled out in the overstuffed chairs and beanbags.

Beanbag chairs ... Amy thought for a moment and then suddenly realized where they were!

"Guys, wake up!" She hissed as she scrambled up and nudged each one awake. "We fell asleep in the Cyber Corner!"

Everyone jumped up and Tiff exclaimed, "My hair! Does anyone have a brush?"

"Forget about your stupid hair!" grumbled Kat. "We have to get back to the cabin before we are caught!"

Amy stood in the middle and announced, "This is what we will do. I will carry the cake, Tiff you get the strawberries and Kat you grab the container of whipped cream."

She turned to Hanna and said, "See if you can fit some forks in your laptop case."

Hanna shoved her laptop into its case and then everyone ran in a circle, bumping into each other while hushing each other to be quiet. They finally had all the items they needed and headed for the door.

"Remember," whispered Amy "if we see anyone, try to hide what you are carrying and act like nothing is wrong."

"If we get caught we probably won't be able to come back next year," whispered Kat. "We've already been in trouble."

"We won't get caught," Amy said confidently. "Let's go."

They shut the door quietly behind them and tiptoed out into the open. The sun was just climbing up over the trees and the sound of crickets was fading. The dew glistened on the grass and there was a chill in the air.

Shivering, Amy led the way. She held the cake in front of her carefully, trying to keep it balanced on the plate. The wet grass was like glass and Amy's bedroom slippers kept sliding as she tried to hurry down the slippery path. Tiff saw her struggling and offered to help.

"Let me carry the cake. I have really good balance."

Amy was relieved as she handed Tiff the plate and took the bag of sliced strawberries. She was happy to let someone else be responsible for the cake.

"Thanks," she whispered to Tiff. "Let's hurry."

## KAT

Kat listened to the sound of their feet squishing through the wet leaves and grass. A door slammed in the distance and all four froze.

"It's probably one of the camp counselors getting up early," whispered Kat.

As they rounded the last bend, a figure filled the path in front of them. A lead counselor stood in front of them with her arms folded across her chest. "Out for a morning walk?" she asked suspiciously.

Hanna stood right in front of Tiff and blocked the counselor's view of the cake with her laptop case. Amy slid the bag of strawberries behind her back and Kat bravely walked up to the counselor with the tub of whipped cream in her arms.

"You caught us," Kat admitted. "We were making instant hot chocolate in our cabin and wanted to add some whipped cream."

Amy played along and added, "We're sorry. We'll return the whipped cream right away."

The counselor relaxed her arms and said, "Oh, don't worry about that. Go enjoy your hot chocolate."

"Thanks," said Kat. "We will!"

## TIFF

The counselor turned and headed down another path as the four reached their cabin. Once inside they collapsed on their beds.

"Oh, my gosh," Tiff exclaimed, "I was so scared I thought I would pee in my pants!"

"TMI!" said Hanna.

"Yeah, that is too much info," replied Kat. "Keep your dirty secrets to yourself."

"Speaking of secrets," Hanna said, "when are we going to give Lily the cake?"

"We need to give it to her soon," said Amy. "We don't have a fridge in here for the whipped cream or strawberries."

An idea came to Tiff as she pictured all the surprise parties she had been to over the past few years. "Let's decorate the cabin!" she said. "We can hang ribbons and blow up some of those water balloons we have left from a few days ago."

"That's a great idea!" exclaimed Hanna. "I can design and print a card. Why didn't I think of that when we were in the Cyber Corner?"

"We can use toilet paper for streamers," chimed in Kat. "I'll go get some from the outhouse."

"I'll start blowing up balloons!" Tiff said.

"Lily will be here to get us for breakfast in about thirty minutes," Amy said. "Let's hurry!"

## HANNA

Hanna hurried back over to the Cyber Corner and set up her laptop. She knew exactly what site to go to for birthday cards. She picked a design, decided on the colors and printed the card.

As she raced back to the cabin, she thought about how much fun she was having. She couldn't believe that a little over a week ago she dreaded going to camp! Now she wished that she could stay all summer!

Hanna opened the screen door and found Kat hanging up toilet paper streamers and Amy tying balloons to the corner of each window. Tiff had her own project going as she tied colorful hair ribbons into little bows and added them to the windows with the balloons.

"It looks great in here! What can I do?" Hanna asked as she caught her breath.

"Can you move the desk to the middle of the room for the cake and card?" Amy asked. "And get the silverware you snuck out in your laptop case?"

Hanna followed Amy's instructions and within minutes, the room was ready.

They each signed the card and wrote a special message to Lily. Then, they all stood in the middle of the room and admired their work.

Hanna looked at her watch and said, "She'll be here any minute."

Right on cue, the screen door swung open.

## LILY

Lily stood in the doorway in shock. They had remembered her birthday! She looked at the cake in Amy's arms and saw that it was an Angel Food cake.

"You guys are amazing," she said as she choked back tears. "How did you know this was my favorite kind of cake?"

"You told us!" Kat said cheerfully. "Remember when we shared our favorite things on the first day of camp?"

"Oh, yeah ..." recalled Lily, "but how did you get this cake? Did one of your moms ship it to you?"

"That's a long story," Amy said as she put the cake next to the card on the small wooden desk. "Read your card so we can cut the cake and have some before breakfast!"

Lily looked again around the room at the white streamers, balloons and bows of ribbons hanging from the ceiling and over the windows.

"You guys are so sweet," she said as she read each line the girls had written on the computer generated card.

"We're sorry we don't have gifts," Tiff apologized as she watched Amy cut and pass out the cake. "It's not much of a birthday party without presents."

"Are you kidding?" Lily said through a mouthful of cake and whipped cream. "This is the best birthday ever!"

"Yeah, but gifts would be nice," agreed Hanna.

"I wish we could at least exchange gifts on the last day of camp," said Tiff.

"I have an idea," said Lily as she poked her fork into another strawberry. "You could put each of your names into a drawing. Then, you draw a name and give that person a "memory" gift. You know, something simple like a feather you found while hiking, something you made, or something you brought with you that you feel someone else should have."

"Yeah, gifts are even more special if they aren't bought at a store," added Amy.

Lily looked around and saw the other girls nodding in agreement so she continued, "Why don't you draw your names today and then think about what you can give that person over the next few days. Then, on the last day of camp you can give that person your gift."

"I think when we draw a name we should keep it a secret until we exchange gifts," said Hanna.

"This is going to be hard," said Kat. "I don't know what to give to anyone."

"Once you draw your name you will think of something," said Lily. "It doesn't matter how big it is, or how unique it is. It just needs to be something that will remind that person of you and their time at camp."

"Like a gift from your heart," added Amy as she tore a page from her journal. "Everyone write down your name and we will draw from Kat's hat."

Lily looked around and thought of how much she would miss each one of these girls. Kat, the tough sarcastic tomboy was actually a sweet girl underneath that tough exterior. And Tiff was no longer so self centered and was starting to think of others instead of just herself. Hanna also changed from a quiet, introverted bookworm to an outgoing, adventuresome friend.

But the camper Lily was most proud of was Amy. Lily recalled how shy and depressed Amy was when she arrived at camp. Lily could tell that Amy had regained her confidence. She was becoming a dependable friend to everyone at camp and now she was acting like a leader in the cabin.

Lily fought back her tears. There would be plenty time to cry on the last day of camp—which was only a week away! Today there would be no tears—just cake, strawberries and lots of whipped cream!

# THE HIKE

## HANNA

Hanna readjusted the straps on her backpack as she gingerly stepped over the rocks and tried to stay on the trail close behind Tiff. They were hiking four miles today with the rest of the campers and they were falling behind. She wished now that she had left her laptop in the cabin.

Hiking was definitely not something she liked. Bugs kept flying in her face and she kept slipping on the rocks. She was also sore from all the canoeing and horseback riding she'd been doing over the past week.

But she wasn't going to complain about horseback riding because that was her favorite thing to do at camp! She remembered how terrified she was the time she had to climb up on the wide back of that humongous horse. But, after a few lessons, it was fun! She loved the horse she rode every day. Her name was Missy and she was so gentle. After she and Missy finished their lesson, Hanna would stroke Missy's soft nose and let her eat carrots and sugar cubes right out of her hand.

Since Hanna had never ridden a horse before camp, she and Missy had to stay in the ring. Once Hanna became a "Trailblazer" she could ride in the woods with the others. Hanna wondered what it would be like to ride Missy on this trail. Suddenly, she bumped into Tiff who had stopped walking.

"Look at all those birds!" Tiff said as she pointed up to the sky.

Everyone stopped and looked up into the bright blue sky at the large flock of birds.

"I wonder why they fly in a V?" asked Tiff.

"Because they are going on a trip and V stands for vacation," Kat said with a giggle.

Hanna hesitated for a moment but then said, "If you are interested in knowing the real reason, then I can tell you."

Hanna could feel that all eyes were on her and Amy responded, "Yes, tell us. I always wondered about that."

"Well," began Hanna, "The latest study shows that birds adopted the V formation for flying long distances because it allows them to glide more often, conserving energy. The aerodynamic V shape reduces the air resistance, allowing the birds to cover longer distances. A flock of geese can fly 70 percent farther by adopting the V shape rather than flying alone."

Tiff stared at Hanna and replied. "You are so smart. How did you know that?"

"I don't know," shrugged Hanna. "I guess I read it somewhere. I'm interested in aerodynamics ..." seeing the puzzled faces, she added, "you know ... flying? I read a lot about airplanes, birds, things like that."

Tiff pulled her sunglasses up on her head and stared at Hanna. "Is there anything you *don't* know?" she asked.

"Well, I don't know much about ..." Hanna thought for a minute and then replied, "makeup."

"I can help you with that!" Tiff said excitedly. "Let's have a makeup party tonight! I brought lots of stuff from my last pageant. I think I might even have some makeup here in my fanny pack!"

"Aren't we too young to wear makeup?" Amy interrupted. "I don't think my Mom will let me wear any makeup until I am like fourteen or fifteen."

"Well, who would want to wear that stuff anyway?" said Kat in a disgusted voice. "I can't believe you brought that clown paint with you on our hike."

"If you put makeup on correctly," explained Tiff in a very grown up voice, "then you won't look like a clown but a beautiful young lady."

"Yuck," replied Kat, "don't make me barf."

"Speaking of barfing," Hanna said, "can we please sit for a minute and rest?" She wiped her forehead and added, "I am getting so hot. I feel like I'm going to throw up."

"I'm hot, too," said Tiff. She then grabbed Hanna's arm and pointed into the woods. "Let's leave the trail and find a cool spot to sit down and I'll show you some of my makeup."

Hanna followed Tiff through the woods and settled in the shade next to Tiff who pulled out a purple mirror and pink lip-gloss. Hanna felt sweaty and gross. She hoped Tiff didn't want her to put on any sticky makeup on her face while they were out here in the woods.

Hanna closed her eyes, sipped some water and wondered how she would look with blue eye shadow on her eyelids and pink blush on her cheeks.

## AMY

Amy caught up with Hanna and Tiff with Kat close behind. Amy didn't need to rest but Hanna did look hot and tired so Amy didn't mind stopping. As she slid off her backpack, she glanced down to the tree where Tiff and Hanna were sitting. A familiar green vine weaved its way up the trunk.

"Um, guys …" Amy said slowly, "you may want to find another place to sit. You are leaning against poison ivy."

Tiff squealed and they both jumped up away from the tree.

Amy looked around at another spot close by to sit but Tiff was already heading deeper into the woods with Hanna. She and Kat followed along as they went further into the thick trees. They hiked down an incline where the ground hid from the sun and the air was much cooler. They veered off to the right around a large tree and kept walking.

The group came to a small clearing. Tiff and Hanna claimed their spot on a large boulder and Kat sat down in the shade underneath the bottom of a large tree. Amy found a soft pile of pine needles and plopped down next to her backpack.

Amy pulled out a small paperback book from her backpack and started to flip through the many pages of animal prints. She loved to find prints on the trail in the woods and then look in the book to find out what kind of animal had been there. She got up and walked in a circle around the area where Tiff and Hanna were sitting.

"What are you doing?" Amy heard Hanna ask.

"Looking for animal prints," she answered and held up the book for Hanna to see.

"Cool …" Hanna said. "Can I look at your book when you are done?"

"Sure!" Amy replied. "I've already found a lot of prints that I can identify from this book. You'll love it!"

Amy noticed that Kat had pulled a baseball from her backpack and was tossing it up in the air and catching it with ease. She wished that she was good at a sport, but she had always been the clumsy one. Kids at school never picked her to be on their team, but the girls here at camp had been really nice to her. They played softball a few days ago with a few other cabins and no one laughed when Amy struck out each time.

At least she was good at horseback riding! She and Hanna both loved to hang out at the stables. Hanna loved her old gentle horse named Missy and Amy love Boots; a three year old Morgan horse with a black glossy coat with white around his ankles. Amy had taken horseback riding lessons before, so she was able to take Boots on trail rides! She wished she could have a horse of her own. Rascal was fun, but you could not ride a gerbil!

Amy thought back to when Lily had called her mom to tell her that Rascal was at camp. Her mom was disappointed that Amy had disobeyed her but she seemed to understand how homesick Amy was and why she needed Rascal to be with her.

Amy smiled when she thought how proud her mom would be right now. Amy had three new friends who made her laugh so much that she almost forgot about being sad!

## KAT

Kat tossed her baseball into the air and thought about the other camps she had been to over the past few years. This was the best camp so far. Her favorite part was still the Blob, and she was so happy that she had convinced Hanna to try it.

Canoeing was fun too, but Kat always had to do most of the rowing. None of her cabin mates seemed to be very strong so Kat had to row extra hard to keep up with the girls from the other cabins. Kat laughed when she thought of the day when Hanna and Amy shared a canoe. They spent most of the time going in a circle in the middle of the lake! But Kat had just been happy that Amy had decided to go out on the lake after all. Amy had changed so much this past week it was hard for Kat to remember how quiet and shy she was when camp first started!

Kat was also relieved that she did not have another episode of sleepwalking. They were so busy all day she was too exhausted to walk in her sleep! She had also limited the number of Hershey bars she ate when they made S'mores. Lily had called Kat's mom about the sleepwalking episode but Kat's mom was cool about it. She just asked if they would put a bell on the door of the cabin so that her friends would wake up if she tried to go outside in the middle of the night.

Kat wondered if her new friends would come back to this camp next summer. They hadn't talked about it yet, but they would need to sign up early if they wanted to share a cabin again.

Kat tossed the ball higher into the air. She would miss this place once camp was over … but most of all, she was going to miss her three new friends.

## TIFF

Tiff was thinking about which makeup would look best on Hanna. Should she try gold or light brown eye shadow? Would peach or pink lip-gloss look best? If she had known earlier that Hanna was open to the idea of makeup, she would have brought more makeup with her on the hike.

But makeup didn't seem to matter at this camp at all. Tiff was just getting used to the idea of just jumping out of bed and putting your hair back in a ponytail. No curling iron, no hairspray and no lip gloss. It was actually somewhat nice not worrying all the time about how you looked!

Tiff wondered if her dad picked out this camp for her. She seriously doubted that her mom would have approved of this camp if she knew how much her daughter would have to be roughing it. But Tiff really didn't mind! Okay, she had to admit that she missed the comforts of home but she was really having a lot of fun.

For the first time, she had made some friends who seemed to like her—not because she was pretty or popular—but because they actually liked being with her! They laughed so much that Tiff almost wet her pants several times! Well, that was also because she still hated to use the outhouse and would hold it longer than she should.

Thinking of using the bathroom, Tiff wondered how long the walk was back to the cabin. She glanced up from her backpack towards the trail when she suddenly had a terrible realization.

"The trail ..." she said in a terrified voice as she jumped up and looked around. "Which way is the trail? I can't see it from here!" A knot formed in Tiff's stomach as she looked in every direction for signs of the trail that led back to the cabin.

Hanna stood up next to Tiff. "Calm down. Just because we can't see the trail from here doesn't mean we are lost."

"We are lost!" Tiff wailed. "I can't believe this is happening. We're gonna die out here in the wilderness!"

Tiff felt Amy's arm around her, "We'll find the trail ... don't worry. And besides, there's nothing out here that will hurt us."

"Yeah, just some bears and wild boars," Kat added in a sarcastic tone. "Let's not sit here and wait to get eaten by wild animals. We need to hurry and get back to the trail."

Kat started walking in between two large trees with Tiff close behind.

"Stop trying to scare me," Tiff said as she tried to keep up with Kat. "There are no bears or boars out here."

"Actually," Amy said as she and Hanna caught up with them, "Kat's right. I saw some boar tracks earlier."

"I can't believe this is happening," wailed Tiff. "This experience could mentally scar me for life!"

"Lighten up," Kat said. "Your head is already messed up from all that goop you put on your hair so nothing can mentally scar you! Just think of this as an adventure you'll be able to tell your grandkids about."

"I probably won't live to have grandkids," cried Tiff. She was really scared. She felt like the tree branches were reaching out to her, trying to drag her further into the deep thick woods.

# The Instant
# Message

**AMY**

Amy didn't mean to scare Tiff but it was true—she did see boar tracks earlier! Not just one set of tracks, but three! The tracks looked fresh which meant the wild pigs could be close by.

"Where are our camp leaders?" Amy heard Tiff whine. "My dad will sue big-time when he finds out I was lost in the woods!"

"It is not the camp's fault," said Amy. "We could've stayed in the cabin while Lily helped out that younger cabin whose leader is sick. We all agreed we could handle this hike without her. We were warned to stay with the group and not go off the trail, remember?"

Amy saw that she had everyone's attention so she added, "I am sure the rest of the hikers have realized that we are not with them anymore. They will be looking for us so we should stay in one place and let them come find us. I feel like we are walking in circles."

Amy stopped walking and was surprised when everyone else stopped and turned to look at her.

"Wow," Kat said in awe. "That's the most words we've ever heard you say at one time."

Amy smiled and replied, "And probably the most important. Let's pick a spot and sit down. I promise you that someone will find us soon."

## KAT

The spot they picked out was right under a tall tree with lots of branches that were begging to be climbed. Kat took one look at the tree and volunteered to climb up and see if she could spot the trail.

"I might even be able to see the camp," she said as she began to swing from branch to branch.

"You look like a monkey up there," she heard Hanna yell.

"And she probably smells like one too!" Tiff added.

"I heard that!" Kat yelled down at Tiff.

"Pay attention and be careful!" Amy yelled.

Kat glanced down and spotted Hanna settling down under a tree and taking out her laptop. What good is a computer out here in the woods?

Kat reached the highest branch that could hold her weight. She stretched out her neck and looked around. All she could see were the tops of trees, miles and miles of green trees. Disappointed, she started the tricky climb back down the tree.

"So, did you see anything?" she heard Tiff yell.

"No," she yelled back down. "The woods are so thick with trees I can't see any trails."

As she reached the last branch, she hung for a few moments from the branch and then let go to land on the ground.

"Ouch!" she yelled as a sharp pain shot up her ankle. She moaned as she realized that she had landed on a large tangle of roots at the bottom of the tree. Her foot was wedged in tight.

Amy was at her side immediately and held her up before she fell over. Tiff also scrambled up the large roots and looked down at Kat's foot.

"You're stuck," Tiff announced.

"Duh.... thank you Miss Einstein for the news flash," Kat said as she winced. "Can you guys help me get my foot out?"

Tiff scowled at Kat for a moment and then ran over to her backpack.

Amy spoke softly to Kat and said, "Can you wiggle it a little?"

"No, my ankle is wedged in tight between these roots."

Kat noticed that Hanna was typing furiously on her laptop. This really irritated Kat so she yelled, "What are you doing? I'm over here in pain and all you can do is play on your laptop?"

"Sorry," Hanna said, "but nursing is not my thing and besides, I'm not playing. I am working on something. I think I might be able to get us out of here."

"With a computer?" Kat yelled back. "What are you going to do—e-mail us out of here?"

Hanna ignored Kat and kept typing when Tiff ran back to Kat with a pink bottle in her hand.

"We don't need her," Tiff said. "I can fix this."

"I don't need to smell pretty!" Kat moaned as she spotted the fancy bottle in Tiff's hand. "You and Hanna are both crazy!"

"Just relax," said Tiff as she started to squirt some of the pink shiny goo down the sides of Kat's ankle.

"Gross!" yelled Kat. "It feels so slimy."

Kat tried to jerk her ankle away from the cold gel and then exclaimed in surprise, "Hey, it's working! I can wiggle my ankle a little! Squirt some more of that junk in there!"

"It's not junk," Tiff said sternly. "It's very expensive oil my mom bought me. It's from...."

"Just squirt some more!" Kat interrupted.

"Fine," Tiff said as she squirted the rest of the bottle down each side of Kat's ankle above her shoe.

Amy gently took hold of Kat's ankle and wiggled until it slowly slid up out of the tight space.

"Whew," Kat breathed a sign of relief as sat down next to the tree, rubbing her ankle.

"I think you sprained it," Amy said with a worried expression on her face.

"Yeah, it's swelling up around my ankle bone," said Kat. "But I'll be okay. I've sprained my ankle before. No big deal."

"It is a big deal!" cried Tiff. "How can we get out of here if you can't walk?"

"Yeah," said Kat as she tried to wiggle her ankle, "I guess you have a point."

Kat then noticed Tiff holding the empty bottle and said, "Wow, I'm sorry you had to use all of your expensive goop on me."

"Well, it's not like I'm going to need any perfumed oil anytime soon," whined Tiff. "Like maybe never—since I'm going to die out here!"

"Just because I can't walk doesn't mean we won't get rescued." Kat said.

Kat winced at the pain in her ankle but took comfort in knowing that at least she wouldn't be bored sitting out here while they waited. Watching Tiff rant and rave would keep Kat *very* entertained.

## HANNA

Hanna watched the drama out of the corner of her eye. She was too busy to stop to help Kat. She knew that Kat would understand once she told them that she had found a way to get them out of the woods.

Hanna looked up from her laptop and announced, "We are going to be saved!"

"What?" Tiff shrieked as she ran and looked over Hanna's shoulder as an Instant Message popped up on the screen.

"You're talking to someone!" Tiff exclaimed.

"Yes," said Hanna. "Like Amy said, I figured we've been walking in circles which meant that we should've still been close enough to the camp office to get a wireless connection."

"So, who are you talking to?" Amy asked as she looked over Hanna's shoulder.

Hanna thought of the secret she had been keeping to herself for months. It was time to share her secret with her friends. Maybe she would even be able to get her mom and dad to accept her online friendship with Alex. He was a good friend, not some weird stranger she had met on the computer. Alex was going to help rescue them!

Still, she had broken the one rule her parents had enforced—no talking to strangers on the Internet. She would need to tell her parents and accept her punishment. But for now, the important thing was to get rescued.

"Well," she began, "it's my friend named Alex. He is online with me right now. I told him how we were lost and he said he would help us."

"Is Alex your boyfriend from home?" Tiff asked in astonishment. "Is he cute?"

"Is he *cute?*" repeated Kat. "What does it matter how he looks? I thought you were worried about dying out here in the woods!"

"I am worried. But I still want to know if her crush is cute," Tiff replied.

"He's not my boyfriend," Hanna said as she took a deep breath, "He is a friend I met online."

## TIFF

"What?" shrieked Tiff as she jumped back. "You're talking to a stranger on the Internet?"

Tiff didn't go on the Internet much. Her mom let her use the computer occasionally to look at the latest teen fashions. Tiff had heard about girls who met guys on the Internet. The guys turned out to be creepy men who wanted to hurt them so she was very careful when she went online.

"Don't you know about *Stranger Danger?*" Tiff asked. "You could get kidnapped!"

"Alex is not a stranger!" Hanna insisted. "He's my friend who is trying to save us and...."

"He can't save us!" Tiff interrupted. "He could be dangerous!"

"Tiff, get real," Kat yelled from her spot under the tree. "He's not going to crawl out of the computer and get us!"

"Well," Tiff demanded as she folded her arms across her chest and glared at Hanna, "How is he going to save us?"

"As I was trying to explain," Hanna started slowly, "I gave him the name of the camp and he called information and got the phone number of the camp office. He is calling the office now to let them know we are okay."

Hanna looked at the confused faces and added, "I would call myself but Lily took my cell phone after Tiff tried to order Chinese food, remember?"

"Yeah," said Kat, "What kind of idiot orders won ton soup for delivery to summer camp out in the woods?"

"I am not an idiot!" declared Tiff. "I was just really hungry. And I am really getting hungry now."

"Let's not fight," said Amy. "I am just glad that Hanna's friend is helping us. Now the camp will at least know that we are okay and won't worry."

"Won't worry?" Tiff exclaimed. "They are supposed to worry—that's their job!"

"Their job is to find us," Hanna said, "and Alex is helping them. He will tell them that they can find us somewhere within the wireless connection distance from the camp. He's already checked, and the service is about a two-mile radius towards the northeast. This information will help them narrow the search so they can find us quicker."

She then added with confidence, "We are going to be rescued soon. I promise."

# THE BOOK

## TIFF

Tiff tried to relax but the trees still seemed to be closing in on her.

"This place gives me the creeps," she said. "You guys keep promising that someone will find us soon but how can you be so sure?"

"I told you," Hanna said. "Alex is letting the camp office know where they can find us."

"I still think it is weird that you have a friend you met on the Internet," said Tiff.

"Alex is the one friend I can depend on to be there everyday to talk to me," explained Hanna. "I'm not popular like you are—with millions of friends at school."

"Well, I don't really have many real friends either," Tiff admitted.

"You?" Kat said with a shocked expression. "Miss Beauty Queen Princess? I thought you had tons of friends and adoring fans!"

"Ha-ha, very funny," said Tiff. "I think people like to be with me because I'm popular. But, I don't think they really *like* me. Do you know what I mean?"

"Well at least people know who you are," said Amy. "I would love to be popular. The kids at school don't even know my name."

"Kids at my school know who I am but no one ever wants to hang out with the brainy girl," said Hanna. "But I guess it doesn't matter since I have study so much. I hardly ever have time to get together with a friend just to have fun."

"Well, girls don't want to hang out with me much either," Kat admitted, "unless they want to flirt with my brothers."

"It's obvious that we all have some serious issues with friendships," Hanna said. "Too bad there isn't a book on how to make a friend or keep a friend."

"There is!" exclaimed Amy. "I saw it at the American Girl Place. The book is called *How to Make and Keep Friends*, or something like that. My mom knows I don't make friends very easily so she gave me a gift certificate so I could buy it. But I bought the stuffed dog named Coconut instead."

"Is there a CD version of this book?" asked Kat. "You know how I hate to read."

"Well, I don't need a book or a CD," said Tiff with a toss of her hair. "It's not my problem that other girls are jealous of me."

"Tiff, you not only need the book *and* the DVD," said Kat, "You need your own fulltime personal 'how to be a friend' consultant!"

Tiff stuck her tongue out at Kat and glared.

"It seems like none of us knows much about making friends," said Amy. "But there are other things we are good at—like surviving this camp!"

## HANNA

"Hey, I have a great idea!" said Hanna as she jumped up and stood in front of the other girls. "We can write a book together on how to survive summer camp!"

"We have to survive this hike first!" Tiff whined.

"I love to write," Amy said, ignoring Tiff's comment. "This will be so much fun!"

"I can help type and format the book on my laptop," offered Hanna.

"What can I do?" pouted Kat as she propped her foot up on a large rock. "I hate to write, I don't know how to type and I can't draw."

"You are ...," explained Hanna as she put her arm around Kat, "our inspiration."

"I'm your what?" asked Kat looking puzzled.

"Inspiration," repeated Amy. "She means that you will give us all the ideas for the book. You are the one with the most experience with summer camps, right?"

"Right," agreed Kat with a smile on her face.

"What about me?" asked Tiff. "If we do come out of these woods alive then I want to help, too!"

"Well," said Hanna, "You like to draw."

"Yes!" squealed Tiff. "I can draw the pictures for the book!"

"I just thought of a name for the book," said Amy with a proud smile on her face, "*How to Survive Summer Camp.*"

"No offense, but that sounds boring," Kat said. "I wouldn't read a book with that name."

"I didn't know you could read," said Tiff with a smirk.

Hanna saw Kat's face glaring at Tiff from under her tattered baseball cap.

"Of course I can read," said Kat. "You're the one who probably can't read. You know what they say about dumb blondes!'

"Very funny ..." Tiff replied.

"Guys, stop arguing," said Hanna. "Let's just think of another name for our book."

"I can't think of anything right now," said Tiff as stood up and crossed her legs. "I can't concentrate."

"Let me guess," Hanna said. "You have to GGP."

"Yes," Tiff said with a frown on her face.

"Just go squat behind those bushes and get it over with," Kat said.

"Gross!" wailed Tiff.

"Yeah, that is pretty gross," agreed Hanna. "The outhouse is bad enough, but peeing in the bushes?"

"She doesn't have another choice," said Amy. "C'mon, Tiff. I will walk with you and stand guard."

"Yes, guard the princess from the raccoons ..."

Hanna interrupted Kat and said, "We are in crisis mode here, Kat. Can you just stop your teasing until we get rescued?"

## KAT

Crisis mode—what did Hanna mean by that? They were just lost in the woods a few miles from the camp—no big deal!

Kat ignored the others and tried to move her ankle. Kat thought of the many times she had been hiking with her family. She was sure she could find her way back to the trail but now she couldn't even stand up without a sharp pain in her ankle. What a bummer.

But, she had to admit that Amy was right. The number one rule when you get lost in the woods is to stay in one place. Kat would make sure they had this important rule in their book.

Kat looked up and laughed a little as she watched Amy and Tiff. Amy stood with her back to Tiff who was standing behind the other side of the bushes. Tiff squatted down and then bobbed right back up as she moaned, "I can't do this!"

With Amy's encouragement, Tiff squatted down again and then back up to moan, "This is so gross!"

As she watched Tiff bob up and down behind the bushes, Kat realized how much she admired Amy. She was always so nice and was there to comfort anyone who needed her help. Like the time Hanna burned the tip of her finger on the hot marshmallow stick. Or the time Tiff swallowed a bug by mistake when it flew into the water bottle. Amy was even the first one by her side today when her foot was stuck. Now, she was standing guard over the peeing princess.

Kat watched as Tiff finally emerged from the bushes and quickly ran back and sat next to Hanna. Amy went to her backpack and rummaged around. She then came up to Kat with a water bottle.

"Here Kat," Amy said. "I just remembered that I had this water bottle in my backpack. It was frozen when we left the camp so it is still pretty cold. You can put it on your ankle to help with the swelling."

"Thanks, Amy," said Kat. "You're the best, and I mean it."

Amy smiled and said softly, "Thanks, Kat."

## AMY

Amy was relieved that Tiff finally went to the bathroom behind the bush and was sitting quietly, for once, next to Hanna.

She sat next to Kat and helped her hold the cold bottle on her ankle. Kat was so brave; she never cried or seemed scared of anything! Amy would love to be as strong as Kat was.

As the foursome sat there quietly, they heard a low rumbling noise above. Amy said a quick prayer for the clouds to blow away.

"It's going to storm!" whined Tiff. "Am I the only one terrified of being out here?"

"No," said Amy as she watched large gray clouds formed in the sky. "We are all scared but the best thing we can do is stay calm."

Amy watched Kat as she opened her backpack and pulled out a large plastic poncho. She was even more surprised when she heard Kat say, "Hey princess, you and Hanna should sit over here. We can all share this poncho and try to stay dry."

Tiff and Hanna scrambled over next to Kat and Amy. They all huddled under the poncho as the clouds opened up and heavy rain formed puddles around their feet. The sun was starting to go down and Amy could tell that even Kat was getting a little worried. Even though Kat loved to tease everyone, Amy knew that she was not really a bully and would always protect and stick up for her friends. That's what the four of them were—friends. No, not just friends—best friends.

"Hey guys," Amy said over the sound of pounding rain, "I thought of a better name for our book."

"Let's hear it," said Hanna.

"*The BFFs Guide to Surviving Summer Camp*," Amy said proudly.

"I love it!" said Hanna. She then added, "You guys are the best friends I've ever had."

"You're my best friends, too," Tiff said. "And, just in case we die out here, I want to tell you that I love you all."

"Tiff, you are such a drama queen. We are not going to die out here!" exclaimed Kat

Kat then looked around at each of them and said, "Okay, I have to admit that you guys are my best friends, too."

"I knew it!" exclaimed Tiff as she hugged Kat.

"Hey," exclaimed Kat as Tiff had her arms around her, "Watch the foot!"

Amy and Hanna joined the group hug and they all huddled closer under the poncho.

Another noise rose above the sound of the rain and they all froze to listen.

"I hear voices!" exclaimed Hanna. "I knew they would find us!"

They all jumped up and started screaming, "Over here! Here we are!"

# THE PLAY

## KAT

Kat sat on her bunk and watched Tiff and Amy practice their song for the play. She had already finished her part as the narrator and had hobbled over to her bunk on her crutches.

They had been practicing every day since their rescue from the woods. Kat had not realized how bad she had injured her ankle until the camp director and counselors had come crashing through the bushes. She was so excited to see them she had jumped up in excitement. The pain that shot through her ankle was so bad she toppled right over into the mud!

It took four counselors to get her out of the woods! They took a blanket, with two on each end, put Kat in the middle, and lifted her up as if she was in a hammock. Kat was embarrassed to be carried out of the woods but it was definitely easier than trying to hobble out while leaning on someone's shoulder!

Kat went to the closest hospital for an x-ray. Her ankle wasn't broken but the doctor said she would need to use crutches for several days until she could put her weight down on her foot. Since she was on crutches, she had to miss many camp activities—no Blob and no horseback riding. Plus, she had to sit and watch the others learn how to line dance last night.

However, she still had fun over the last few days because Mrs. Donavon let Kat be her assistant in the camp office! She answered the phone, helped file forms in the campers' folders and even helped pick out the menu for the dinner for tonight before the play! Kat picked her favorite—Barbeque Ribs, Corn on the Cob and Baked Potato! For dessert, she chose Peach Cobbler with Vanilla Ice Cream.

Tonight she would use her crutches to hobble across the stage to a stool where she would sit and tell the story about two young witches who met at a boarding school. At first, they couldn't stand each other but, despite their differences, finally became friends. Just like us, thought Kat as she looked across the cabin at her new best friends.

## HANNA

Hanna sat with her laptop on her bunk bed with iTunes playing the song "Popular." She had also downloaded scenes from the actual Broadway play. She then cut and pasted the photos into a Power Point presentation that she would show on the large screen at the back of stage during their performance.

The other girls were so amazed at the things Hanna could do with her computer. Hanna was thrilled to show them how to create animation, download videos and a lot of other cool stuff. She still could not believe that some schools didn't even offer a Technology class!

Hanna thought back to the day they were lost in the woods. Her laptop saved them! Without her computer, she would not have been able to contact Alex. When she sent him the Instant Message she was so thrilled to see that he was online and able to help them.

What she was most excited about was that her parents didn't freak out when they found out about Alex. Her parents were so happy that Hanna was safe that her mom actually called Alex's mom and told her how much she appreciated his help. But, her mom had told Hanna that they would have a long, serious talk about Internet safety when she returned home.

Hanna stood up to scratch the back of her legs. She was so itchy from the terrible rash she and Tiff both had on the back of their legs after they sat on poison ivy. The camp nurse gave them both a cream to use but the rash was spreading to her arms now.

Thank goodness, I don't have to be on the stage tonight, Hanna thought to herself as she scratched the back of her arm. I wouldn't want anyone to see me with an awful red rash.

## TIFF

Tiff looked over and saw Hanna scratching at her arm.

"Hanna," she said, "stop scratching. You will only make it worse."

"I can't help it!" Hanna said. "I can't find my tube of anti-itch cream."

"I think you put it in your laptop case but here," she said as she walked towards her with a small white tube in her hand, "you can use some of mine."

"Thanks. My rash is getting worse. Look—it's spreading to my arms!" Hanna cried.

"Well, no one can see my rash since it is just on the back of my legs and I am wearing a long dress," said Tiff. She twirled around in the long pink gown that she had found in a trunk of costumes the camp used for skits. Another camper who was a Fairy Godmother in a skit a few years back had worn the dress. Tiff thought it was perfect for her role as the Good Witch of the North.

Tiff was so excited about the skit that she had almost forgotten about her traumatic experience in the woods. She had never been so frightened in her entire life! But her friends had been there for her—even Kat. Tiff knew now that Kat would never stop teasing her but she also knew that Kat would always been there if she needed her.

## AMY

Amy still couldn't believe she had a part in a play! Tonight she was going to be on stage in front of the entire camp! She was a little nervous but excited at the same time.

She really didn't have to perform or anything. She just had to sit there in a chair while Tiff danced around her and sang while she brushed Amy's hair and pretended to put makeup on her. Amy was the Wicked Witch so she would already have green face paint all over her face and her arms and would wear a long black robe and witch's hat.

"Who has all the props?" Hanna suddenly asked. "We need to make sure we have a hairbrush, a mirror and Tiff's makeup."

"Do you really think the princess would go anywhere without her makeup?" Kat asked. "Amy, I still can't believe you are going to let her put some of that stuff on you!"

"I told you, she's not really going to put it on me," explained Amy. "She is just pretending to put make up on me."

"Well, I was thinking of at least putting some lip gloss on you," said Tiff. "For real, not pretend."

"See!" exclaimed Kat. "You can't trust her!"

"I am more trustworthy than you!" yelled Tiff.

"You are not!" Kat yelled back, "You always do whatever you want without asking other people first!"

"Oh, like you actually ask permission before you do everything?" Tiff asked.

Here we go again, Amy said to herself. She was really going to miss all of this commotion. What would she ever do without these three best friends?

# THE FAREWELL

## HANNA

Hanna woke up with the back of her legs starting to itch again. She was still tired from all the excitement last night but she couldn't sleep anymore with her itchy skin.

Her last night of camp was so much fun! The girls in every cabin did a great job with their performance but their cabin won 2$^{nd}$ place for the best skit!

Hanna could not believe she would be leaving camp today—the past two weeks had flown by so quickly! She couldn't imagine not seeing Tiff, Kat or Amy for another year. They would have to find a way to get together before next summer. Maybe they could all meet for a weekend! She wondered if her parents would let them stay at her house.

Once the rest of the cabin was awake she would ask them about planning a BFF reunion. In the meantime, they could keep in touch by e-mailing each other. Kat said she was getting a cell phone soon so they could text each other! Hanna couldn't wait to give Kat her gift—she had drawn her name and had the perfect gift for her!

As much as she would miss camp, she was happy to see her mom and dad again. She smiled when she thought of the dad's comment about the potholders. This camp was not that lame! They didn't make stupid potholders but learned how to make cool stuff like dream catchers and tie-dye shirts. Hanna laughed aloud when she thought of Kat who tie-dyed her white sports bra!

## KAT

Kat was awake and thinking about how hard it was going to be to say good-bye to her friends. She had never met friends like this before. Even though they were different from each other, they all got along great! She even had to admit that she liked Tiff. Never in a million years would she of thought that she could be good friends with a prissy spoiled princess. The more she had gotten to know Tiff, the more she realized that Tiff was funny and sweet and very amusing!

Kat heard a giggle from across the cabin, "What are you laughing at?" she hissed.

"You!" was the reply from Hanna's bunk.

Kat climbed out of her bunk and padded in her bare feet across the floor. She quickly climbed up onto Hanna's bed and sat at her feet.

"Okay, what's so funny about me?" asked Kat.

"I was just thinking of how you tie-dyed your white sports bra on craft day," Hanna said with a giggle.

"Yeah," Kat replied as she started to giggle too. "I wonder what my mom is going to think when she sees it! She should be happy that at least I'm wearing a bra!"

"I have idea," Hanna said in a serious tone. "Let's plan a reunion during winter break."

"That's a great idea!" agreed Kat.

They both pondered the idea for a few more seconds when Kat said excitedly, "That's about the time you will be finishing up your sports league so maybe we can come and watch your final game!"

"And you will be done with Etiquette School so you can serve us tea and cookies!"

They both fell over laughing when a flashlight shone in their eyes.

## TIFF

Tiff woke up to the sound of laughter and grabbed her flashlight. She knew it wasn't a ghost this time so she didn't hesitate to jump out of her bed and join the fun.

"What's going on?" she asked as she climbed up next to Kat.

"We are planning a BFF Reunion!" announced Hanna.

"Cool! I love reunions!" said Tiff. "My mom's side of the family has these huge reunions every year where we all wear the same t-shirts."

"Forget about matching shirts," said Kat. "No way!"

"Well, we also sing songs and play games on the beach," suggested Tiff.

"Thrilling," Kat replied. "Our reunion will blow your mom's gig away."

"Well, what do *you* want to do at our reunion?" Tiff asked Kat, "Oh wait, let me guess … play basketball?"

"Great idea," Kat said with a grin.

"No way," said Tiff.

"Let's wake up Amy," said Hanna, "and then we can all talk about our ideas for the reunion."

"But first let's exchange gifts!" suggested Tiff.

"Finally," Kat said directly to Tiff, "you actually came up with a good idea!"

## AMY

Amy was deep in sleep when she felt someone pull off her blanket.

"Wake up!" Hanna was yelling. "It's our last day of camp!"

"Yeah," added Kat. "We have some plans we want to talk to you about!"

"And we want to exchange our gifts!" said Tiff.

Amy sat up and stretched. She looked at her three cabin mates with their messy hair and big smiles. She felt her eyes tear up as she thought of how much she was going to miss them.

"Thinking of your dad?" Tiff said gently as she saw her tears.

"No," Amy said she shook her head. "I was thinking about how much I'm going to miss you guys!"

All three climbed into Amy's bed and they had a group hug.

"Okay," Kat finally said, "enough of the mushy stuff. Let's exchange gifts and then Hanna has a great idea we want to talk to you about!"

"Presents, first!" said Tiff as she ran to her trunk and opened the lid.

Hanna and Kat also ran towards their trunk but Amy simply reached under her pillow and pulled out a small flat package wrapped in newspaper.

The three climbed back up into Amy's bunk and they sat in a circle.

Tiff handed a box to Amy. "I hope you like it."

Amy unwrapped the pink tissue paper and opened the box. Inside were Tiff's prized possession.... her white Chanel sunglasses.

"Tiff!" she exclaimed. "You know I can't accept these. They are your favorite and they are way too expensive!"

"They are my favorite pair but you are one of my favorite friends so I want you to have them," Tiff said sincerely.

Amy leaned over and gave Tiff another hug. "Thank you so much. I love them and I will take really good care of them!"

It was Amy's turn so she handed the small package to Hanna. She watched as Hanna unwrapped the gift and found Amy's book of animal prints.

"OMG!" Hanna exclaimed. "This is the book your dad gave you!"

"Yes," said Amy. "But I want you to have it. I know by next summer you will have the whole book memorized and we can have fun tracking animals!"

"You even wrote a message to me inside," Hanna said softly.

"Read it out loud!" Kat said.

"Okay," said Hanna, "It says.... *Friends are hard to find and tough to leave. Hoping we stay best friends forever, Love Amy.*"

"That is so sweet," Hanna said as she leaned over to give Amy a hug. "Thanks so much."

"Okay, princess," Kat said to Tiff, "here is something you desperately need. I just hope your Mom doesn't burn it."

"Burn it!" Tiff said in a shocked voice. "Why in the world would she...."

Tiff tore off the paper and shrieked in glee as she held up Kat's tattered Clemson University t-shirt. "You're giving me your favorite shirt!" she exclaimed as she held the shirt up to her cheek. "I love it!"

"My turn," said Hanna as she handed an envelope to Kat.

"You gave Kat money?" asked Tiff.

"No," said Hanna. "You'll see."

Kat tore open the envelope and unfolded the sheet of paper. Her eyes grew wide as she said, "Wow, you wrote down your text message codes!"

"Yes," said Hanna. "I wrote down as many as I could remember. Now when you get your cell phone we can send messages to each other all the time and your brothers won't know what we are talking about!"

"Awesome!" said Kat as she gave Hanna a high-five.

"Okay," Amy said to Hanna, "tell us your idea."

Hanna explained the reunion and they all agreed they should plan it around Hanna's final game and Kat's completion of etiquette school.

"I'll talk to my parents about it on the drive home and then e-mail you guys a message," Hanna said.

"If you can't have it at your house maybe we can have it at mine!" Tiff offered. "My birthday is in December so you guys can come during Winter Break!"

The door opened and in walked Lily. They all ran to her with their gifts and Lily listened to the story behind each one.

Finally, Lily said in a serious tone. "It's time to pack up. You need to eat breakfast and then your parents will be here to pick you up."

## LILY

Lily stood on the gravel road and waved good-bye to her campers. She brushed away a tear with the sleeve of her shirt and then kept on waving.

She smiled as she saw Amy's face lean out of the window of the red pickup truck wearing those huge white sunglasses with a grin on her face as she held Rascal in her hand. A horn honked and Lily heard Kat yelling TTFN out of her car window. Hanna added to the commotion by standing up through sunroof of her car and waving wildly. Tiff had her chauffeur drive in a circle while she blew kisses to Lily out of the rear window of the limo with her bunny KeeKee cradled in her arm.

Lily kept waving until the last car disappeared through the wooden gates.

She stood by herself for a few minutes and said a quick prayer to guide them home safely. Lily knew in her heart that she would see them again next summer. She may not be their counselor next year but she was certain that the girls would make their way back to camp and end up in the same cabin. She even heard them talking about getting together again before next summer!

Lily turned to walk back to the empty cabin. She missed them already. Kat, Tiff, Amy and Hanna … best friends forever.

# APPENDIX

▼

## Hanna's list of Text Message Codes

| | |
|---|---|
| ASAP | As soon as possible |
| BFF | Best Friends Forever |
| BOOMS | Bored out of my skull |
| FUBB | Fouled up beyond belief |
| GGP | Gotta go pee |
| G9 | Genius |
| JK | Just kidding |
| NBD | No big deal |
| NFM | Not for me |
| NP | No problem |
| OMG | Oh my gosh |
| SLAP | Sounds like a plan |
| STW | Search the Web |
| TA | Thanks alot |
| TTFN | Ta Ta for now |
| YW | You're welcome |

978-0-595-47683-1
0-595-47683-X

Printed in the United States
119328LV00001B/250/P